MW01016044

VENUS BUTTERFLY

ANONYMOUS

Carroll & Graf Publishers, Inc.
New York

Copyright © 1989 by Carroll & Graf Publishers, Inc.

First Carroll & Graf edition 1989

Carroll & Graf Publishers, Inc.
260 Fifth Avenue
New York, NY 10001

ISBN: 0-88184-489-6

Manufactured in the United States of America

VENUS BUTTERFLY

CHAPTER 1

This is the story of The Lily.

But it is really the story of the *Yoshiwara*. For The Lily and the *Yoshiwara* were each typical of each other. You could not think of the *Yoshiwara* without thinking of The Lily. She *was* the *Yoshiwara*. Externally cold, with the hauteur of a queen, she was, nevertheless, a warm person and quite human, too.

But first, for the benefit of those readers who are unaware of the fact, the *Yoshiwara* is that district in Tokyo, the capital of Japan, that is set aside for the segregation of the Houses of a Million Pleasures. The English, as unpoetically as ever, bluntly term them whorehouses. In America, where I traveled for some time, that particular section is known as the

Red Light District, or the Line. In Japan we call it the *Yoshiwara*.

But this humble scrivener hastens to inform the reader that, in no way, is there a similarity between the *Yoshiwara* and the Red Light District. The American system makes a sordid thing of prostitution, hence it is forced to exist in sordid surroundings and outside the law. But the Japanese, saturated with the wisdom that comes with years of philosophical contemplation, see in prostitution the natural outlet for man's natural excess of sexual emotions with his leanings towards vicarious extramarital pleasures. Therefore, the *Yoshiwara*, in distinct variance to its American counterpart, is located in the most beautiful section of the Japanese countryside. In fact, the value of the land of the *Yoshiwara* is four times as much as ordinary Tokyo business property.

Let us take, for instance, the *Shin-Yoshiwara*, which is the newest of the six *Yoshiwara* of Tokyo. This section is in the northwestern outskirts of the city and is about an hour's *jinriksha* ride from the main busines section of Tokyo. You enter through a wide gate. On one side of the gate is a weeping willow tree, the Willow of Welcome. On the other side stand two policemen, *Yoshiwara* policemen, for the necessary evil is under the supervision of the government. The streets inside the gate are long and wide and are lined with alternating teahouses and shops. Down the middle of the street is a flower garden, resplendent with gorgeous growing blooms. It is about six feet across and is interspersed with rock gardens and quaint stone lanterns. Miniature figures are placed among the flowers of the rocks.

From the eaves of the peaked, bamboo roofs hang two rows of red lanterns. And two rows, likewise, run down the sides of the buildings. At the end of the street is a large building with a clock tower on it that dominates the entire scene. Similar buildings with stone fronts are found scattered around the other streets that branch out from the main street. Lofty pillars on the wide verandahs and high, vaulted entrances abound, through which can be seen cool, green gardens extending beyond great staircases.

Such, as you see, is the *Yoshiwara*. It is something beautiful to behold. And the women with whom we enjoy a few short hours of blissful pleasures are, likewise, beautiful to see. That is why the story of The Lily, of her life in the *Yoshiwara*, to us Japanese, is really a sad and a beautiful story. And that is why I, who have traveled over the Western World, and have learned the customs and the languages, have been commissioned to write this beautiful story of a beautiful *oiran*, The Lily.

The Lily was the *oiran* in an *o-mise* of the *Shin-Yoshiwara*. This means that she was the highest class of prostitute in the section. Her clients were composed of men who could afford to pay her well. And they realized that in the Lily, they were obtaining the services of no ordinary *zaro-soba* of the *Sagami* provinces, or *goke* of the *Hokkaido* district.

In fact, as I now write about her, I find that I must draw considerably upon a few sparse observations of my own together with the few things that I have been told by others. For very little was really known of The Lily. Of her forebears, one can only conjecture. But, undoubtedly, somewhere far back in her genealogical history, there was some white blood. For, strangely enough, her eyes were not as slanted as those of most of our Japanese women. And her hair, although it was pitch-black, was not straight, but had a distinct wave in it and was of a silky texture. But, most of all, she had a marvelous complexion. Japanese women cannot boast of this. They cover their faces with white powder so that they are almost a deathly white. This closes up the pores of the skin and thus brings blemishes to them. But The Lily had as fresh a complexion as a rose. And although her face was very white, one could still discern the faint tinge of shell pink coloring her cheeks.

But the Lily's charms were not only confined to her complexion. Of medium height, every part of her body was perfectly proportioned. Japanese women's hips are usually too high, thus destroying the perfect line of symmetry that joins their torsos with their limbs. But The Lily's hips were as symmetrical as the petals of the flower after which she was named. Two little breasts jutted out from her bosom like twin apples on which perched twin teats of pink. When she walked they did not shake like ungainly waterbags but undulated gently like a shaken leaf. At the point of the triangle of her hips one could see nestling in a charming mass of curled hair, the shapely

12

cunny that had made her name ring throughout the entire country as the most dexterous whore Japan had ever seen. And, despite the thousands of fuckings that her little cunny had enjoyed, instead of being terribly distended as one would expect, it pouted out as though it were the delicious quim of an unfucked virgin whose maidenhead still reposed safely on the bottom of her lovespot. Other famous whores had offered her thousands of *yen* in return for her secret. But she steadfastly refused to divulge her secret to them. So that, after fifteen years of constant fucking, when I myself found my penis entering her vagina, I swear that I experienced the same tight pleasures, the same inexorable sucking feeling as I had felt when I had first fucked my little cousin, a girl of twelve. The moment the head of my prick touched the aperture of her cunt, it seemed as though a tremendous suction seized my member and drew it unceasingly into The Lily's cunt. Then I felt a strange tugging sensation, as though my stiff prick were being milked by tiny hands. And this went on for almost five minutes. And all the while, The Lily lay back on her quilts, her eyes closed, her hands clutching my body and her fingernails digging deeply into my flesh. And her ass moved around spasmodically. But all the while I could feel the powerful but tiny muscles in her cunt contracting and tightening so that I felt that the very life blood was being milked from my veins.

I go so much into detail about my own personal experiences with The Lily so that I might be able to explain better the reason for her having reached the pinnacle that she enjoyed in the *Yoshiwara* at Tokyo. For, in all my days, I can truthfully state that never, never had I been fucked as I was fucked by The Lily. During my travels, I made it a point to visit the most notorious whore in every town that I visited. Literally, I have fucked thousands of whores. Yet only once did I ever come across one who could be compared to her. It happened in New Orleans, I believe, in the U.S.A. During the carnival season I made the aquaintance of a young Creole girl in the Mardi Gras, which is a great street dance where people dress up in costumes and masks, somewhat like we Japanese do on certain feast days. This semicolored girl was only fifteen years of age. She had not been broken. But I paid her father who introduced me to her a pretty penny and, for that, I received the privilege of breaking her maidenhead. Somehow she had the same faculty of contracting her cunt muscles as did The Lily. And, in her passion, while she was moaning like a hurt child, I could feel my prick within her quim pulsating like the heart of a trapped rabbit. Usually I am able to withhold my coming for about a half hour's duration. But her milking, her exquisite fucking made me blow my bag of cream after five minutes of piquant poking. And she, the Creole, likewise came with me, so hot was she with passion. And, our lips glued together, our tongues exploring each other's mouths, I felt my prick grow soft within her cunt. But, wonder of all wonders, as I lay in bed with her, I felt that strange, insisting pressure of the walls of her vagina against the sides of my already softened penis. And, with the same sucking and milking action of her cunt muscles, she slowly worked my prick up to another hard-on within five minutes, without my finding it necessary to withdraw. Again the child moaned in pain and pleasure, as my stiffened member tore ruthlessly at her already torn and bloody maidenhead. But, despite the obvious pain, she almost swooned with pleasure in my arms. Almost swooned I say, for I knew that she was still conscious enough to direct those wonderful muscles in her cunt to continue their milking action and thus make me blow off again much sooner than I was accustomed to doing.

* * *

But enough of this Creole. The story of which I must write concerns The Lily. And, later on, I discovered that she had the same faculty of milking the male member as the Creole had. But she went the Creole two, three and four times better in that she was able to cause a stiff prick to harden within her cunt, not only once, but twice and three and four times. And, with the enormous wrestler, rumor has it that she was fucked by him fifteen times! But for that I must wait until I reach that time in her life. First I must start off when she was yet a child.

In Japan, when a girl child is born, the father bewails his fate at first, resigns himself to what must be and, straightaway, forces his wife back to the marriage bed, hoping this time that she will deliver a boy to him after nine months. Girls are not thought much of here. And so it was when The Lily was born. But none knew who The Lily's mother and father were. She simply had appeared on earth. That was all. And the earliest record of her is found in the police entries for new prostitutes. Listed there were a few facts, namely, that one *Mikawa-ya* desired to take The Lily into his establishment, known as the *jimpu-ro* or simply, Number 9. As it is necessary that each new whore have a sponsor who sells her services to the brothel, it was found that the name of the sponsor was *Kobayashi*, a commoner who kept a curio shop in the *Naka-dori*, that street which runs parallel to the main thoroughfare between *Kyobashi* and *Nihon-bashi*, that is full of shops where old curios and brocade are exposed for sale.

It seems that one day, when the *Naka-dori* was filled with people, a beautiful young female child had wandered into *Kobayashi's* curio shop. The curio dealer, an unmarried bachelor, a rarity indeed in Japan, eyed the intruder gruffly and sought the doorway for the child's parents. But no parents came. Meanwhile, the child was curiously examining the dusty earrings and jewel boxes and spangles that littered the floor.

"Where are your parents?" the dealer asked.

The child merely shook its head from side to side and eyed the gruff countenance of the man above her with mild attention. "I have no honorable parents," the child lisped, and in her eyes there appeared a strange look, the same look the one poet-lover of The Lily called, "queenly-majestic."

"Then who brought you here?" the dealer asked.

"*Ogawa*," the child replied naively.

"Who and where is this honorable *Ogawa?*" the dealer asked.

The child half-turned and indicated the stream of people milling past the curio dealer's shop. "There is *Ogawa!*" she said and, without another word, with the manner of an emperor who had given his last word in an interview, the young girl turned to the curios and gave her attention once more to the brightly colored objects.

The girl remained with *Kobayashi,* the curio dealer, for the rest of the day, but no *Ogawa* returned to claim the lost child. That night, after closing up his shop, *Kobayashi* made another bed for the girl, determined that the next morning he would hie himself to the police station and there return this nuisance of a girl who happened in so suddenly on him, disturbing his bachelor's peace with her calm, level stare that seemed to probe within the very innermost recesses of his soul. Somehow, whenever he talked to The Lily, he felt that she saw through all of his lies and false posturings. The moment a lie came to his mouth, he thought he could see her lips curl faintly in a derisive smile and her eyes would level themselves calmly at him. And he knew that she was laughing at him. During my travels in France I once saw a picture called *The Mona Lisa,* and the woman in it had the same sort of curl and smile on her lips that The Lily used to have. It gave an otherwise nunnish set of features the faint semblance of a whore. And, likewise with The Lily, it gave her the looks of a nun, a holy woman. So that, when one fucked her, one felt that one was fucking a nun. One felt that one was ravishing the hitherto unravished portals of a beautiful recluse who had set herself aside for God. One felt, in fact, that one was making God a cuckold by fucking his personal whore. That is why The Lily was so popular a fuck among the Japanese. No matter how many encounters she had had previously, always the present one seemed like the first one to the man. For, the while he skirmished around the delicious, quivering lips of her vagina, he could see, or rather he thought he could see in her face, the composed mien of an unfucked girl.

* * *

But, to The Lily's early story.

When *Kobayashi* awoke the next morning and found the little girl in his own bed next to him, he looked down at her sleeping face and stroked a wisp of hair away from her eyes that had dropped away from her head. Even in her sleep there was the same curl around her lips and, although her eyes were closed, he felt that she was staring levelly at him. The next moment, she opened her eyes and smiled a good morning up at him with her eyes.

"Good morning, honorable sir," she vouch-safed up at him.

He was about to rumble something rough at her but, instead, he replied, "Good morning to you, oh glorious child of the sun!"

Again she smiled brightly up at him. "I'm hungry," she said.

He rested on his elbow and looked down at her. "Who are you?" he asked.

"I was *Ogawa's*," she answered, "but now I am yours, oh honorable man. What is your honorable name?"

"*Kobayashi*," he answered, "and yours shall be The Lily from now on. How old are you, Glorious Lily?"

"Twelve."

Something within the body of the man beat a fearful tattoo within him. Deep within his bed quilts he could feel the soft body of the girl-child brushing against his own naked limbs. He lifted his hand and rubbed it against the bosom of her nightgown that he had salvaged from one of his own. Beneath the cloth he felt the scarcely rounded outlines of her breasts just barely expressing themselves.

"Are you not afraid of *Kobayashi?*" he asked her slowly.

The Lily looked up at him through her eyelids. The cool, leveling stare came into them. The curl of a smile played around her mouth. "No!" she said simply, "I fear not my honorable master, *Kobayashi*."

"Has any man ever touched you where I touch you?"

She shook her head.

Kobayashi's breath now came in short, labored gasps. His groping hands now went under the cloth of her nightgown through the open collar. His hands caressed her breasts lovingly. Then he slowly drew the quilt away from them and threw it back on the floor. Both of them lay open now. Beside his long hairy legs, he saw her slim body, like coral carving outlined under her nightgown. He looked into her face once more. The same calm expression was there. She was absolutely untroubled. She seemed to know what to expect next. And when *Kobayashi's* quivering hands went slowly to the hem of her gown and drew the bottom away from her white body and left it bare to his eyes, she still stared unconcernedly at him, the taunting smile evident around her lips.

Kobayashi's eyes almost popped out at the sight of her delicious bare body lying next to his. He examined her thin thighs that were as shapely as carved ivory. Now he could see her breasts. They were twin mounds of alabaster, scarcely nubile, yet emitting an unmistakable feeling that they were to be for man's pleasure rather than for his use. As she lay on her side, the powerful swing of her hips sweeping down to her flanks from her buttocks foretold of the beauteous form that was to come. Then he looked down at the slit between her legs. Only faint hairs scattered themselves around it. But it was so small that it could scarcely be seen. With a hesitant finger, *Kobayashi* touched the pouting lips.

"Has any other man seen you as I see you

now, oh honorable Lily?" he asked, a quaver of passion disrupting the even tenor of his voice.

She shook her head and smiled. "No other man has seen or had my beauty," the child said with the words of a woman.

In reply, *Kobayashi* sank his head down between her thighs and sniffed the delicious virgin fragrance of her vagina. Unspoiled, unravished, he knew that here was a prize that would be his for only a short time.

"Spread your legs a little," he begged of her.

She did as she was bid. *Kobayashi* saw the tiny lips of her quim extend slightly as she drew her limbs away from each other. And, glistening slightly in the center of the lips, he saw a pinkish spot appear. *Kobayashi* could control himself no longer. With a deep moan, he buried his head between her legs once more and began to move his tongue furiously between the lips of her tiny cunny. Around and around the tip of his tongue probed. And when it came to the projection of her clitoris, his tongue wrapped itself insinuatingly around it so that it stiffened and grew almost a quarter of an inch.

Instinctively, without being told what to do, The Lily began to move her bottom around with a circular motion. And, at times, she gave her cunt a thrust forward as though she were trying to work his tongue further and deeper into the recesses of her vagina. And a delicious series of moans issued from her. And her eyes took on a sort of mad stare. And her mouth opened and closed as though she could

21

control its movements no more. And her tongue laved her lips as though they were parched dry. Her hands reached down to *Kobayashi's* head and, as it bobbed up and down between her legs, she pushed down heavily as if to make him sink his tongue deeper into her throbbing cleft.

"I cannot stand it any longer!" she cried.

Kobayashi drew his head away from between her legs. "May I love you as you should be loved?" he asked of her, and it appeared as though he were a lowly slave begging a favor of an emperor. And as she talked, he fingered the little button of her clitoris all the more so that it stiffened again.

"Do something, honorable sir!" she moaned, "do something . . . do anything!"

In answer to this plea, *Kobayashi* hastily tore away his own nightgown and displayed his prick projecting ominously between his legs and, like a haltered stallion, raring to be let loose. "This shall soothe thy passion, oh illustrious Lily!" he whispered to her as he jockeyed himself between her legs and prepared to enter her tiny cunt with his enormous prick.

"What are you going to do?" the girl wailed now.

"I am going to make you a woman!" *Kobayashi* replied, and he spread her legs as far as he could so as to separate the lips of her cunt as much as possible.

The Lily closed her eyes and awaited the first violent thrust expectantly. Suddenly, she felt something enormous brush up between her legs. Then she felt as though a great tree were being rammed up into her very belly. "Don't!" she cried out in pain. "Don't!"

But *Kobayashi's* passion was far too much for him to have stopped his ranting prick now. He went slowly at first, knowing that he was ravishing the virgin cunt of a girl. But even this slowness was too much for her. Within her, she could feel the tearing onslaughts of a monster ripping away her innards ruthlessly, rending her flesh into tatters. But somehow, behind the excruciating pain of ravishment, she could sense a strange feeling of well-being, a strange emotion like the one she felt when *Kobayashi* had thrust his agile tongue into her throbbing hole like lightning. And her breath now came in short gasps. And her clenched fists gripped her palms so tightly that her fingernails imbedded themselves into her flesh. And the muscles of her ass, of their own accord it seemed, suddenly took on all of the motions of fornication, and received his body thrust for thrust so that he no longer found her an unwilling recipient to his enormous prick.

But best of all, he began to feel an unusual sort of sensation around his swollen penis. Somehow or other, little hands were stroking it, as though they were milking the teats of a cow's udder. And, under these ministrations, he felt his cock harden even more until it finally reached a point where it could stretch no more. The sensation of milking was a delicious one. It was the muscles in her cunt that were doing it, he knew. What a marvelous woman she will be, he thought to himself as

23

he busied himself with burying, withdrawing and burying his penis into her bloodied little hole.

Before he realized it, he felt something in him give way. He was coming, he knew. So he threw himself down over The Lily's tiny body and began to kiss her eyes and lips and breasts madly. The Lily seemed to sense what was the right thing to do, for she seized his tongue in her mouth and rolled it around there. Suddenly she felt something very hot splash against the sides of her vagina. It seemed to warm up inside her entire body. Then, wonder of wonders, she felt something within her own body release itself and a lush, warming sensation enveloped her like a blanket of pleasure. And her legs ceased their terrible threshing and relaxed. And the lips of her cunt ceased their violent throbbing and pulsated faintly. Within her, she could feel the once hard prick of *Kobayashi* soften gradually until it became as soft and as pliant as a kitten. Over her whole body, through her tired limbs, in every joint, despite the lacerating pain that seared her vagina, she could feel a gentle, soothing stream of supreme happiness and joy creeping insidiously over her.

From then on, The Lily knew what she was to live for.

CHAPTER 2

That day, *Kobayashi* left his little curio shop
for the police station. But not for the same
reason that he had originally intended. Instead
of reporting to the captain that a girl-child
had strayed into his place of business, he stated
that his brother's daughter, one *Ogoro*, had
been brought to his humble domicile because
of the death of his brother in the far off
Satsuma province. Therefore, he humbly pe-
titioned that she be, from that day on, his
adopted daughter.

And so *Kobayashi* became The Lily's uncle,
although he did not act as most uncles do toward their nieces. Rather he was more her
husband. For every night, after he closed his
shop, he would repair eagerly to the little alcove

at the back and there sip sake that The Lily had prepared for him together with a delicious meal of fish, rice and eggs.

And after imbibing the liquor, his brain awhirl from the alcohol, he would draw The Lily down to his bed on the floor and there enjoy her infinite plenitude of pleasure such as he had never experienced before. He taught her the subtleties of fornication. For twenty years, having had an aversion to marriage, he had been a regular client of all of the brothels in Tokyo. And from the thousands of *yuyo*, *oiran*, *shogi* and *joro* he had fucked, he had taken away some individual mannerism that had added to his pleasures, some twist of the ass or peculiar modification in a fucking position that each whore practiced.

All of these variances in the ancient art he taught to The Lily. Night after night, he would draw her down, spread her legs wide apart and start in on the education of a whore. And the while *Kobayashi* demonstrated his arts to her, The Lily would look at him quizzically, as if to say, "why is this funny little man pushing me about so like a puppy nuzzling a bone," and she would lie acquiescent to his every demand but, all the time, remembering every minute detail of the instructions in fucking that her adopted uncle was teaching her.

It was *Kobayashi* who first discovered her ability to use the muscles in her cunny to such an advantage. It happened about a week after The Lily had strayed into his shop. *Kobayashi* had spent a hard day in his shop. English tourists had crowded in and out and all of them

had been hard bargainers and kept him sometimes for an hour piddling over a neck charm
with the great shrine of *Narita* carved on it,
arguing down to the last *kotsu*, than which
there is no smaller amount. And so, after having spent a hard day in the shop, *Kobayashi*
had dragged his weary feet to the back room
where reposed his Lily, awaiting him with a
hot bowl of sake and rice but, best of all, with
open arms in his bed.

Although his body was tired, the alcohol in
the sake stimulated his mind. So, as he stared
down at The Lily, lying gracefully in bed, he
pushed away his bowl of rice and sank down
to the floor on the quilts.

"Honey-lily," he whispered to her while he
undid the *obi* that Japanese women wear continually about their waists.

"What does my most honorable master desire of The Lily?" she lisped provocatively to
him, and she tried to edge herself away as
though she were trying to avoid his fumbling
fingers.

"Your most humble slave desires you," *Kobayashi* continued, and he drew the *obi* away and
threw The Lily's kimono open. She did not
bother, ever, to wear the customary Japanese
articles of underclothing beneath her kimono.
There were no *koshi-maki* and *suso-yoke* loin-
cloths, *noshita-jime* belt; nothing, only her
own delicately colored skin gleaming up in the
candlelight like age-old parchment. Her white
body stood out from the background of her
dark-blue kimono like a white heron against
the background of night.

Kobayashi could only gasp at the beauty of the girl's body. Wonder of all wonders was woman's body, he thought. And as his thoughts roamed, so roamed his eyes up and down her body, resting at times at certain lovespots, admiring this tiny curve and that, stroking this nook and that. And as he looked, he felt his own sexual member begin to rise beneath his own dressing robe. And he cast his robe away from him and, with a deep moan, threw himself on the waiting girl. But she pushed him away.

"Thy honorable tongue first!" she demanded imperiously, and she spread her white limbs and prepared her cunt for the intrepid explorations of his tongue. *Kobayashi* dropped his head between her proffered legs and sent his fiery tongue darting upward into her already throbbing pussy. Studiously, he avoided touching the button, skirmishing meanwhile in every other possible part of her orifice.

"The button, the button!" The Lily demanded, seizing his head in an attempt to force him.

But *Kobayashi* only grinned and refrained from licking it until finally, when he felt that she could stand the ordeal no longer, he suddenly seized the tiny lovespot in his mouth and began to suck gently on it. It grew harder and longer and with this change, a change came over The Lily. Instead of lying acquiescent now, she was a mad animal panting with heat and eager for the onslaughts of the male member. Back and forth she moved her ass and cunt as though she were trying to work his busy tongue deeper into her vagina.

"Have me now!" she cried. "Now, before I spend my essence in vain!"

Swiftly, *Kobayashi* drew his head away and leaped on her, dangling his already lengthened prick ominously in front of him. For a moment, before inserting it into her throbbing cunt that seemed to be gasping for contact, he rubbed it around her already stiffened clitoris.

"In! In!" The Lily moaned.

And *Kobayashi* sent his rampaging prick straight into her cunny, deep into her cleft to the hilt, so that the hairs around his prick mingled now with the few pubic hairs that were scattered around her hole. Before that time, *Kobayashi* had contented himself with using the usual method of poking his prick in and out of her cunt, in and out, using the friction of the flesh to bring them both to their passion's height. But this time, somehow or other, *Kobayashi* determined to let his prick remain in her cunt and let her wiggle her ass and slide her cunt up and down over his prick.

"Move up and back!" he commanded her.

But The Lily was oblivious to his commands. She knew only that in her there rested the most delightful thing in the world. She knew only that coursing throughout her entire body was a fiery essence that suffused her brain with warmth and made her every nerve tingle with suppressed joy and excitement. She knew only that in her was the stiff prick of a man. So she heard not his command to move but contented herself with pulsing wildly in passion. Then, without any conscious volition on her part, she felt a peculiar movement in the region of her cunny. Suddenly, she discovered that she could control the movement. When she so willed it, the movement of the muscles stopped. And when she willed otherwise, she could make the muscles move like mad. She did this for some time, noting the response of these movements in the eyes of *Kobayashi*.

He, meanwhile, had received the most pleasant shock in his entire fucking career. As he lay quietly in her, waiting for her to go through the fucking movements, he felt the most peculiar movements around his stiff prick. Hands, little hands it seemed, were stroking his penis the while it reposed in The Lily's taut cunny. He was being milked, he felt. The sensation was excruciatingly delicious. It was as though she had taken his prick into her mouth and was sucking, sucking on it, drawing out from him his vitals, the very essence of life, draining his loins of everything.

"What are you doing, oh beloved one?" he asked excitedly.

She stared up at him. Now she knew what she was doing. She was conscious that she held still another secret in the ancient art of fucking.

"More, more!" *Kobayashi* insisted, and this time he could not control himself any longer and started to work his prick up and back into her hole, as though his very life depended on it. And, as he manipulated his penis into her cunny, she meanwhile worked her newly found muscles the more, straining herself to the utmost in an attempt to manipulate them.

"I can stand it no longer!" *Kobayashi* blurted out. "I must spend my seed!" And spend he did, spurting his fluid into every crevice of her vagina. And, the moment he did so, The Lily let herself go and together the two warm fluids mingled in her hole and overflowed through the crevice so that it streamed out and covered her entire front with its pearly warmth.

For the moment, *Kobayashi* was too stunned to go through with the rest of the fuck. Instead, he allowed his prick to grow limp within her warm, fluid-flushed cunt while the afterfuck sensations coursed out of his lions and into his entire system. Beneath him, The Lily panted from exhaustion, the lips of her quim quivering, tiny globules of fluid teetering on the hairs around the shell-pink cunt-lips. And then, as though she desired to withdraw the spent prick entirely within her hole, she started the muscle movements again, sucking mightly at the limpid member like a drowning man sucks for a few free breaths of air. Then, to aid her in her attempt to bring *Kobayashi* to a hard-on again, she started to move her hips and buttocks in a circular motion, taking care that his still-soft prick would not slip out of her eager hole.

And then, still leisurely resting in the afterthroes of the last fuck, *Kobayashi* felt his member slowly come to life. Again he felt the soothing, stroking sucking motions of The Lily's cunt muscles grasping and regrasping his prick, tugging and tugging at it, trying to stiffen it once more into activity.

"Marvelous Lily!" he whispered into her ear, and he bit it playfully. And when he felt life stir once more within his prick, he began to help her and started to shove up and back, gently at first, so that, in a short while, it had again retained its former virility and now stood stiffly at attention, like a soldier awaiting the call to duty, to discharge his gun at the proper moment.

All the while, The Lily worked the marvelous muscles in her throbing cunt, knowing that soon she would be able to bring her man up to a point where he would again spurt his warm seed into her and inundate her innards with its enervating fluidity. And, in back of her little head, she noted the reactions of the man and knew that she possessed something that was priceless. Again it happened. Into what seemed the most vital section of her body, where all of her nerves seemed to be fused into one, where all of her emotions were as one great emotion, The Lily felt *Kobayashi's* fluid creeping like a warm flood of honey, insinuating itself into every crevice, oiling every tired muscle, soothing every jangled nerve, draining every tired feeling from her body. And she lay wearily and panted from passion and labor and felt *Kobayashi's* lips fall onto her own lips and smother them with kisses. And she kissed him back again and again, hoping that he never would stop kissing her or fucking her.

Lying on top of her, his prick still in her pulsating cunt, *Kobayashi* hoped that he never would lose her. But, deep down, he knew that soon he would have to lose her. He was getting old. He had already fucked himself out in the *Yoshiwara*. The fire was gone. Now there was only sparks. Now there was only the mighty flickering of the last few dying embers. And then there would be darkness. Then there would be no more fucking. Then there would be no more of The Lily. His head sank to The Lily's breast. He wept.

"Why do you weep, honorable master?" The Lily inquired anxiously of him.

Kobayashi lifted his head and stared at The Lily's calm features through the tears in his eyes. He saw her only as a blur. He said nothing. He only knew that his doom was sealed, that his scroll was soon to be rolled up and laid away to gather dust.

The Lily thought that he was weeping because of her. She had not satisfied him, she thought. He was weeping for her. With almost superhuman effort, she strove once more to stimulate his lagging passion with the potent muscles in her vagina. Busily, she inserted her tongue into *Kobayashi's* mouth and kissed him again and again while she contracted her muscles and stroked his penis with sure strokes; whirling her ass and cunt around so that, with the movements in her cunt, it was not long before *Kobayashi's* prick had almost regained its rigidity for the third time. Round and round The Lily whirled her buttocks. Suddenly, the man's penis slipped out from the grasp of her avid cunt. Hastily, The Lily seized it. Without losing a moment, she lowered her head and popped it into her mouth. Up and down her head went, her tongue inside her mouth rubbing the entire length of the prick as it darted in and out of her mouth. *Kobayashi*, meanwhile, had regained his former desires. He saw that The Lily was striving mightily to please him. So, he drew her over to him and inserted his finger into her hole and began to frig her button, at the same time taking the delicate little nipples of her slight breasts into his mouth until they stiffened with passion.

"Now!" he called out as he felt his member stiffen.

The Lily straightened herself out and spread her legs for her master. In, deep and firmly, went *Kobayashi's* prick. And as it sank deeply into her, The Lily began to work her muscles up and back. Up and back shot the mighty prick into The Lily's distended cunt. Round and round whirled her ass. Up and back in conformity to *Kobayashi's* pokes went her buttocks. Loose and tight went the tiny muscles in her flaming cunny. Madly, mightily, both of them lost themselves in an overwhelming frenzy of passion. Their lips found each other's lips. Their hips whirled in unison. Their hands sought each other's bodies, stroking their parts fondly.

And then they came into each other.

After that, without drawing his softened penis from her wildly throbbing cunt, *Kobayashi* felt a drowsiness creep over him. And he fell asleep, his head sinking between the young breasts of The Lily.

The Lily lay back and marveled at life and its joyous opportunities.

* * *

Perhaps, oh honorable reader, you wonder
why I linger with such detail upon these earlier
experiences of The Lily. Allow me to inform
you that the psychology of a whore is both
simple and complex. For those *shogi* who become ladies of pleasure for the money, the
reasoning is simple. But there is a kind of
shogi who does not enter into her profession
because of monetary remuneration. Something
in the life itself, somthing in the constant fucking of myriads of men, something unknown
to themselves even, compels them to follow
their age-old professions.

So it was with The Lily, I believe. It was
her destiny to be a whore, as much as it was
the destiny of his most royal highness, the
emperor of Japan, to be the *Mikado*. And it was
a combination of her own natural talents,
coupled with what she learned from *Kobayashi*,
coupled with her own natural inclinations, that
made of her what she was, the most dexterous
whore in Japan.

But, to return to the earlier history of The
Lily.

For two years, The Lily remained at the
household of *Kobayashi*, during which time she
catered to his belly and his prick. But, as the
days drew into weeks and the weeks into
years, the old fellow began to discover that the
girl was too much for him. Nights would come
when, after one fuck, he would have neither
stamina nor desire for another. And still later,
as he feared, he began to lose desire even for

that one. Naturally, as the desire lessened in the elderly person, the desire increased in proportion in the younger. Nights would find The Lily moaning in anguish, weeping her heart out because her lord and master could not satisfy her lust, her mad desire for more fornication. And, to cap it all, she reverted to something that decided once and for all, for *Kobayashi*, that The Lily was for him no more.

It occurred during the waning days of the second year.

All during the night, The Lily had worked over the limp penis of the old man. From the moment he had let himself drop gently onto the quilts, she had tried with all her myriad arts to revive the manhood in him. She took his prick into her mouth and sucked violently at it, tickling his balls the while with one hand and inserting her finger into his anus and massaging his prostrate gland with the other. She kissed him passionately, which is rare for the Japanese, for they seldom, if ever, display affection in that manner. She inserted his prick into her avid cunt and attempted, through muscle manipulations, to bring the thing back to some semblance of hardness. She massaged it with the palms of her hand, kissing the tip at intervals, and took it entirely into her mouth again in exasperation when the aged prick showed no signs of revival. Finally, in desperation, she burst into tears and turned away from the bewildered *Kobayashi*.

There was nothing that the old fellow could do. He had spent himself in one grand flare of fucking for the last two years. He was burned out now. He merely stared at the heaving shoulders of the young girl and tried to compose himself for sleep. Finally, when he did manage to fall asleep, he slept for only a short while. For suddenly, as though it were a dream, he thought he felt motion in the quilts beneath him. He opened one eye. He saw The Lily seated at the side of the bed. Her legs were spread wide apart. Her breath was coming in short gasps as though she were experiencing the most passionate of orgies. But, shame of shames, *Kobayashi* saw that she had taken the candle from the candlestick and had inserted it into her throbbing cunt. In and out she shoved the long dildo, and as she sank the thing deeply into her crevice she would give a moan and her whole body would quake spasmodically, and the tears would spout freshly from her eyes.

With his one eye open. *Kobayashi* stared shamefacedly at the actions of the distraught girl. He saw her occasionally stop the candle and tickle her clitoris. His mouth watered at this. He determined that, for the last time, he would satisfy this girl, if it took all of his willpower and manpower to do it.

"Lily, beautiful blossom!" he cried out as he threw the quilt away from himself. "Dry the tears from thine eyes. I shall gather together the spent forces of aged bones! I shall fuck thee for the last time!"

With these words, he seized the candle from out of her quivering hands and threw it away from him, as though it were anathema to him. Then, with a sigh, he lowered his head and dropped his face into the delicious cleft that yearned so anxiously for his manhood. Deeply, luxuriously, he sank his pointed tongue into her anxiously awaiting cunt. And, the moment The Lily felt the contact, her hips gave a mad, wild heave and she attempted with her violent motions to make his agile tongue touch every aching corner and nook. Moan after moan came from her lips. She felt the old man's fingers go around her nipples. She felt them tighten. She felt the old man's tongue coil itself sinuously around her clitoris. She felt it tighten. She felt a furious boiling sensation in her groin. She felt her button grow in size as the blood rushed amorously to it. She stared up at the ceiling and experienced once more the pleasurable tortures of passion.

"Have me, have me!" she cried to him.

But *Kobayashi* found that, despite the ardor that he had used in licking her cunny, his prick still dangled impotently in front of him. In a rage of anger, he seized the lifeless thing and tried to force it into the palpitating lips of her cunny. But it was to no avail. He could only touch her button with its head, and it seemed to hang in shame because of its ineptitude. Suddenly, a thought came to *Kobayashi's* head. The while he frigged The Lily with his finger, he extended his hand out into the corner where he had thrown the candle and retrieved it from its resting place. Then, with a wild cry, he called out, as though in passion:

"It rises, Lily! It rises!"

"Ah, master!" she wept, "let me kiss its little head!"

"No! First let me show it the duty it must perform!" he replied as he prepared to sink the candle deep into her pussy.

"Sink it now before I faint with pain!" The Lily demanded, and she closed her eyes and resigned herself to the old man. She felt the head of his prick skirmish around her gaping cunny. She felt her sensitive clitoris react to its insistent pressure. But when she felt the entrance of what was supposed to be his prick she gave a great sigh. It was the candle, she realized. But the candle was better than nothing. She would let him believe that she did not see through his deception. She would throb passionately to its caresses as though it were real flesh. And she let her feelings go in a flood of emotion. And the old man, the candle in his hand, his hand pumping back and forth, wept salty tears. And as he saw The Lily heave her loins in response to his probings with the candle, he determined that this was going to be his last night with her. He must give her to a young man who would be a real lover to her, who would fuck her when she wanted to be fucked and as many times as she wanted to be fucked.

He stared down at her beautiful pink cunny. He took a last look at the few hairs that were scattered around its tiny entrance. He touched her clitoris lightly and, sighing as old men sigh, he sank his head once more to her cleft and kissed her clitoris a whistful good-bye. Then he reinserted the candle and worked at its poking again. Finally, The Lily came. She felt her whole insides go out in one grand burst of gigantic passion. And, although she knew that it was only a candle, she was thankful she had been able to get rid of the burden that had tormented her so.

"Ah, honorable old one!" she lisped, "what is to become of me, thy Lily?"

Kobayashi wiped a tear from his eyes. "On the morrow, we shall find a strong young man for thee, Lily!"

"I want no strong young man!" she said suddenly and angrily.

The old man regarded her troubledly. "But I am too old for thee, beautiful flower!"

The Lily pouted beautifully. "I want to be *geisha* girl," she said finally, "for then, then I shall get much money for my services and all the money shall go to you, honorable master!"

Kobayashi tried to object strenuously. He told her what she was to expect as a *geisha*. But The Lily would not listen to him. Instead, she closed his mouth with a kiss and, with their lips still together, their nostrils breathing in each other's breath, they both fell into a deep sleep.

CHAPTER 3

If whoring is the oldest profession in the world, then procuring is the second oldest. Where there is a prostitute there is always some person, particularly an old woman, who knows how to exploit the charms of the girl. Over the rest of the world, the procurer is looked upon with shame. But in Japan, where many things are topsy-turvy in regard to the Occidental aspect, the *zegen* or professional procurer is sanctioned by the government and is required to take out a license in order to conduct his trade.

Muro-matchi was such a procurer. Japanese people are very short, seldom growing over five feet, but *Muro-matchi* was so small that he looked like a dwarf. You could never tell from looking at him that he dealt in human bodies, in the beautiful bodies of young girls. There was ever a benign expression on his face, and were he to dress like one, he could easily have passed for a *Shinto* priest. One felt that when he took an interest, everything was sure to come out right in the long run. He seemed to exude confidence. All of these facial attributes aided him considerably. A young girl, on being brought to him, need not quiver and quake over her predicament. Somehow or other she felt that this kind old gentleman would take care of her and would see to it that she would not suffer any harm. But, in reality, *Muromatchi* was a beast. Every *geisha* and *goke* that he placed in the *kemban* or central office to which prospective clients apply for *geisha* services, or in the *hikite jaya,* had to be first examined by him. His excuse was that he, being the first one to know her, must explain to her the life she was going to lead. But, perhaps it would be better if I explained first just what a *geisha* girl is.

The *geisha* girl can be compared to the Occidental cabaret singer and dancer. From childhood, she has been taught by the *geisha* master, who has purchased her from her parents, how to practice *gei,* which is the art of dancing with hand movements, and singing sad Japanese ballads and conversing wittily with the men who hired her for the night. Whenever a group of young blades desires to have a party, they lease a room in a popular teahouse and hie themselves to the *kemban,* where they put in an order for three *geisha* girls. When these girls arrive at the party, their jobs are to dance, to play the *samisen*, to sing, to tell witty stories and to pour tea for the guests or, more likely, sake, which is the heated juice of fermented rice. Ostensibly, her only duty is to cater to the man's aesthetic and gastronomic senses. In fact, she is expressly forbidden by law to practice anything but certain prescribed things, among which fucking is absolutely forbidden. There is a considerable fine and imprisonment supposed to be given to any *geisha* who has been arrested for fornication. But this law, like many laws in the topsy-turvy land of Japan, is seldom adhered to. The *geisha* girl, like her sister prostitute, will sell her body willingly, providing the guest has sufficient money. She is a *jigoku*, an unlicensed whore, as much as is the ordinary *yo-taka*, or night-walker, or *jigoku-onna*, or hell-woman, who carries her mats strapped to her back and, for a few cents for the night, is ready to lay down in any sewer or ditch, legs spread wide apart, her hole twitching for the contact. The only difference between the *geisha* and the *shogi*, or licensed prostitute, is that where the *shogi* is forced to remain within the confines of the *Yoshiwara*, the *geisha* is at liberty to go where she pleases, wherever she is sent by the central bureau.

* * *

It is necessary that the reader be informed as to the status of the *geisha* girl, because our heroine became a *geisha* shortly after the time that our last chapter ended. *Kobayashi* awakened the next morning to find The Lily combing her long black hair into a fashionable coiffure.

"Why does my Lily sing so?" he asked of her sadly.

"Because she is soon to be a *geisha* girl," The Lily replied gaily. But when she saw the sad look in the old man's eyes, she immediately dropped to her knees and began to comfort him. "I shall remain here the rest of my years if you so will it, honorable master!" she insisted.

"No," the old man replied, stroking her hair, "the fox to his hole, and the lily to its vase!" And with these words, he arose from his quilts and began to prepare himself for the street. "I shall go see my friend, *Muro-matchi*," he said, "who is licensed to procure girls for the *geisha* masters and the *Yoshiwara*. White thy face well. Black thy eyes with *kohl*. Put up thy hair into a likable knot. For I take you with me." And, after saying these words, he shuffled about the room, purposely delaying his departure so that he could remain with The Lily as long as possible. Finally, when he could procrastinate no longer, he gave a deep sigh and beckoned to the awaiting Lily.

"Come!" was all he said, and he left for the door that opened into the street. The Lily followed respectfully a few paces behind him.

They walked down the *Naka-dori,* where all the curio shops were centered. Then they followed a series of winding streets. Finally they emerged into another narrow street. On the corner stood a hotel, a two-storied building with a balcony around the second floor.

"Here is where my friend *Muro-matchi* conducts his honorable business," the old man said gruffly as they stopped in front of its entrance. He looked over the eager countenance of The Lily. Then, taking her hand, he squeezed it gently and led her into the doorway of the hotel.

Muro-matchi was inside to greet them personally. He made the usual signs to *Kobayashi* but when his eyes fell on The Lily, the lower jaw of his mouth dropped and he gaped at her.

"Since when have you, a bachelor, been enriched with such a charming daughter?" he asked of the curio dealer.

"This is The Lily," *Kobayashi* replied, "the daughter of my deceased brother in *Satsuma*, whom I adopted two years gone."

"Charming!" *Muro-matchi* beamed, and he pinched The Lily's cheeks playfully. "But what would you desire of me, honorable *Kobayashi*? It is almost two years since I have catered to your needs. Where have you been? Perhaps . . ." and he stopped at the word, his eyes dropping once more to The Lily. Then a look of comprehension came into his eyes. "Ah!" he said blandly, "I see." Then, as though everything was clear to him now, he asked, "How much, honorable *Kobayashi*, how much?"

"Were I not in need of money for my shop, *Muro-matchi*, The Lily would remain in my household. But . . ."

"But how much?" the procurer demanded craftily.

They finally arrived at a price satisfactory to both. The amount for an ordinary girl was about 20 *yen,* or ten dollars. But anyone could see, even *Muro-matchi,* that The Lily would make no ordinary *geisha* girl. And so he finally offered and gave *Kobayashi* the sum of 50 *yen.* "You have been paid well, *Kobayashi,*" he said to the curio dealer after the papers had all been signed.

Kobayashi looked at the procurer from under his eyelids and smiled grimly. "Your bargain, honorable procurer, is much better than mine." And he arose from the floor where the inkpot and brush lay and prepared to leave. "Come Lily," he said to her as she sat quietly in the corner watching the negotiations for her body with calm eyes and not seeming to care that the two men were bargaining for her.

Muro-matchi broke in as The Lily arose to leave with *Kobayashi.* "She must remain the night here with me, *Kobayashi!*"

"But the law, what about the law!" the curio dealer objected. "The law specifies that under no condition must the prospective *geisha* remain overnight in the house of the procurer."

"I shall take care of the police," *Muro-matchi* replied, as he put a paternal arm around The Lily's shoulders. Then, cupping the Lily's chin in his fist, he lifted it so that her head fell backward. "You can trust an old man like *Muro-matchi,* can you not?" he asked of her.

The disdainful curl appeared once more in

The Lily's mouth. And the mocking smile came into her eyes. "Yes," she said simply.

"You see," *Muro-matchi* said to *Kobayashi*. *Kobayashi* looked from the procurer to Lily. Then, without another word, he turned sorrowfully and pattered out to the street on his sandals. And, strangely enough, The Lily felt no sad feelings now. Instead, she felt that she had risen a step on the ladder. Instead, she felt that there were bigger things, better things ahead. And she smiled her little smile at the procurer.

"Are you really not afraid of me?" he asked her.

She shook her head. "I am afraid of no man," she said, "for I shall give to all men that which they desire of me!"

"M-m" was all that the procurer said as he rubbed his hands together, like a shopkeeper who has just made a good sale. "Then come with me, come with me," and he started to lead The Lily up the stairs that led to the upper balcony floor. "Upstairs, I have a room full of pretty kimonos and long, flowering *obi* for your waist, in a flowering chrysanthemum pattern, and lined with silk such as pretty young girls like you enjoy wearing, and long hairpins for your hair, and *geta* for your feet. Come," he motioned to her, and The Lily followed ,her eyes aglow, her body anxious to don the rich siks and things the procurer had pictured to her.

Once in the room, the procurer turned around and closed the door behind him. "Here is where the pretty things are," he said. Then he edged over to The Lily. "Come, beautiful flower," he said, and his words quivered from his mouth, so great was his passion for the new girl, "I shall help you dress in your new attire." With these words, he took hold of her *obi* and drew it out of its knot so that it fell in a heap at her feet. Then he drew open her robe. Underneath it, The Lily was naked. No underclothing, no hideous clothes of any kind, only her smooth, bare body glistened out as the revealing flaps of her robe were drawn aside by the procurer's trembling fingers. Tremulously, The Lily's beauty of form and body shot out at the old rake like a shaft of sunlight in a cave. In two years her body had taken on more of the characteristics of a woman. Where her tiny breasts merely juted out from her chest before, now there were two shapely globes that would have put the Greek Helen of Troy's breasts to shame, so perfect were they in their lines and elegance. They seemed to quiver with life, on springs of unexcelled vivacity. Lower down, her thin torso flared out into two wings of as shapely a pair of hips that had ever adorned a woman. But best of all *Muro-matchi,* the procurer, saw the jewel that was her cunny, glistening from behind a vail of curled hair that seemed to be an ideal resting place for so glorious a gem as her cunny was. The pink, pouting lips faintly edged with hairs were so small that one thought that they were adorning the cunny of a girl of twelve, so tiny was it, yet so perfectly shaped. For a full five minutes *Muro-matchi* stared entrancedly at the vision that had displayed itself before his eyes.

He felt a catch coming into his throat. Fifty years ago, when he was still a boy, the same catch had come into his throat when he had fucked the first girl. And now, now this slip of a girl was able to recreate the lost ecstasy of that first fuck. The thoughts of the past brought back the desires of the present. He felt strange stirrings coursing up and down the limp length of his penis.

"Lily," he whispered softly to her, "there is work here for us to do."

"Thou art my master," she said naively to him. "What do you want of me?"

Taking her hand, he led her to the bed of quilts that lay prepared on the floor. "It is long since passion has stirred in me," *Muro-matchi* whispered, hardly able to speak louder, so intense were the emotions that seethed within him. Then he drew her down to the bed. Without a word, she spread her legs wide for him so that for which he yearned so mightily. Hesitantly, he reached his hand out and touched the pouting lips. Instantly, the flesh recoiled at the contact.

She lay back on her pillow, eyeing him with expectancy. But still *Muro-matchi* desisted from entering her. "Why are you waiting?" she asked calmly of him.

But *Muro-matchi* was ashamed. Although the desire for her was strong in him, still there was only a slight hardening of his dangling prick.

The Lily looked down at him as he opened his gown. She saw his anemic prick hanging lifelessly like a dead soldier. Reaching over to him, she seized it and stroked it gently, starting slowly at first but gradually working up to a fast climax. But all she could get out of him was a slight rise. Faster and faster came his breath. But it was of no use. *Muro-matchi's* played-out cock refused to rise to the occasion.

The Lily grew desperate. As she worked over the limp member of the old man, she felt her own emotions gradually piling up. Her own breath started to come in short gasps. And, as she stroked the man's prick, he was frigging her with his finger in an attempt to revivify his own flagging emotions. And occasionally, with quivering fingers, he would fondle her breasts or rub her buttocks or kiss her all over the body.

But it was to no avail. There Lily lay, her whole body aching for contact with the man with whom she was lying. And there, with her, lay the man, his entire body aching to enjoy this delicious woman whose beauty was such as he had never before seen, yet he was unable to bring on an erection so that he could enter her.

"What shall I do?" he wailed at her.

But The Lily was now almost beyond reason in her passion. Eagerly she seized hold of the prick and popped it into her mouth. Then, with cunning tongue movements, she stroked the cock's tip and sides in her mouth while she moved her head up and back.

"What shall I do?" the old man continued to wail as he saw that any more effort on her part was useless.

"Get me some man to fuck!" the Lily gasped out as she strove mightily to withhold herself from coming futilely. "Get someone, anyone, so that I may not waste the precious passion that burns me so!" And there was scorn in the last words, and her lower lips curled and her eyes hardened.

Muro-matchi got up hastily from the bed. "I shall get you a man!" he called back as he opened the door. Then he called out loudly, "Chang . . . Chang!"

From the bottom of the steps came back the reply faintly. "Yes, master!"

"Come up here!" *Muro-matchi* demanded. Then he turned away and watched the pitiful antics of the young girl on the bed, squirming in the throes of the pain that comes with unrequited passion. "I shall have a man here for you!" he moaned to her as he laid himself next to her, "a real man!"

The Lily did not answer him but to herself she prayed that he would come soon.

In a moment, the door opened slowly. In the doorway stood a gigantic Chinaman, his lower jaw dangling idiotically open, his hair matted into the semblance of a pigtail, his enormous paws of hands dangling at his sides like an ape's.

"What does the master want of me?" he inquired.

"Take out your staff and see what you can do with this lady!" *Muro-matchi* demanded. "Hurry! Hurry!" he cried as the peasant Chinaman gazed with wonderment at the delicious feast of woman lying there before him. Never before had he seen such a sight. Slim, graceful, cool, her white body was so much different from the peasant women he usually fucked. All he could do was to stand in the doorway and gawk. Then, when he heard his master's impatient cry, he shuffled to the bed on which the beautiful apparition lay outsprawled. His eyes were on one spot only and they seemed to bore their way directly into the aching aperture. Unconsciously, his hands went toward the spot. And his eyes grew wide with emotion. And his tongue slobbered over his lips. And a weakness came into his knees such as would come after a strenuous job of lifting had been done.

"Out with thy prick, fool!" his master commanded.

The Chinaman did as he was bid. But when he drew out his prick, this time The Lily's eyes widened when she saw its enormous length and breadth and heft.

"How is that, Lily?" *Muro-matchi* asked, turning to her.

"Let him take me now!" was all she could say and her hands went out to the hulking brute. Intuitively, Chang pushed his great tool forward and, the moment The Lily's tiny white hand curled around it, it immediately shot out like an arrow from a bow so that it almost doubled in length. Then he dropped on his knees at the entrance to The Lily's gaping hole.

"In, in!" The Lily gasped, and she tried to guide the awful thing into her cunt while her lips gasped for a contact. Chang leaned forward, gently inserting the tip of his prick into The Lily's little hole. Eagerly, lasciviously, old

Muro-matchi took in every detail of the fuck. Faint stirrings of passion once more began to evidence themselves in him. "Lean hard, lean hard!" he admonished the Chinaman. And the Chinaman leaned hard so that his prick began to distend The Lily's hole almost to its utmost. In, in and in went the rapacious prick, insistently pushing its way forward. And when he thought that he had given her enough of it for the time, Chang gently withdrew it to the tip. Then, once more he sent it's entire length hurtling into her body.

The Lily could only lay back on her pillows and moan. Never before had she been fucked by so enormous a prick. Within her there seemed to be a great pole poking her this way and that, seemingly tearing her apart. A cold sweat was pouring from her forehead. Her fingers clutched the bedclothes nervously as the Chinaman continued to insert and withdraw the thing. Faster and faster she felt herself being fucked. And within her there burned a great desire. Until, when she felt that she could stand it no more, she cried out to the Chinaman, "Enough, enough!"

But it was to no avail. The beast in the Chinaman had been aroused. Up and back he continued to ram his rod into the quivering quim. His eyes popped even more now. His hands, great hams, had gone to The Lily's breasts, and were stroking them excitedly. His mouth remained open, the saliva still dripping from his lips. All he could do was mutter in a strange gibberish.

"Stop . . . stop!" The Lily screamed.

But the juggernaut rode on.

Finally The Lily came. And the Chinaman felt a great load in his balls suddenly release itself and squirt into the girl's hot cunt. And, watching the entire proceedings, *Muro-matchi* laved his lips with his tongue and felt that he, too, had shot his manhood into the recumbent body of the girl.

For a while, Chang allowed his soft prick to remain in The Lily's hole. Suddenly, *Muro-matchi* called out, "Go, you fool!" and, sorrowfully, the Chinaman withdrew his penis from the heaven that it had found for itself and backed away to the door while he adjusted his prick into the folds of his blue trousers. And as he backed out, he could not keep his eyes off The Lily's body.

On the bed, The Lily had closed her eyes. Once more that delicious sensation of afterfuck was suffusing her entire being. And, although she felt as though a rope had been pulled speedily between her legs, as the medieval torture artists had done to captive women, she did not mind the pain of having her cunt stretched to almost twice its normal size.

Muro-matchi stared at her. Then he rubbed his palms together.

"Ah, fair Lily," he said slowly, "tomorrow we take you to the *Yoshiwara*."

"There I will become a *geisha?*" The Lily asked.

But the old procurer laughed. "We shall see, little flower, we shall see," and he got up from the bed and padded softly to the door. "Meanwhile rest yourself for the night, so that tomorrow morning, you shall appear clean and fresh and beautiful."

With these words, he turned and left.

And The Lily, her mind now in a turmoil, lay back on her pillows, a variety of emotions disturbing her.

CHAPTER 4

The next morning, when The Lily awoke
from a deep slumber, she discovered upon
opening her eyes that she was in a strange
room. But this did not bother her for very
long. As she stretched her arms and yawned,
she recalled the events of the evening before.
And she smiled her strange smile. And she
rubbed her hands over the tiny hill of dreams
that topped her little cunny.

As she lay outstretched on her bed of mattresses, she wiggled herself out of her night-
kimono and then from between her two padded
quilts so that she was entirely naked. Then she
arose and, seating herself on her knees before
the mirror, she began to admire herself, stroking the soft flanks of her hips, testing the

resilient spring of her breasts, slapping the firm flesh of her buttocks. Then, changing her position, she spread her legs wide apart and, in the mirror, examined minutely the region of her inner vagina. Although there were still traces of redness remaining, still and all there were no signs of the awful ravages that had taken place in the vicinity the night previous. The same round little hole was there blinking perversely in a sort of pearly dew. The same little button was set cockily above like a corporal's hat. The same pink flesh surrounding her love spot was fresh and alive like newly-cut cherry blooms.

It was good to be alive, she thought, as she resumed her position on the bed her arms outstretched her eyes closed to the seven shafts of sunlight that were shooting in through the open *amado* which she had thrown open. Over her entire body she felt the warming rays send pleasant waves of warmth.

She heard the sound of *zori* on the stairs.

Muro-matchi entered. In his hand he held a tray on which was a bowl of tea and some little cakes. *"O hayo gozaimas!"* he vouchsafed in morning greeting to The Lily.

"O hayo!" she returned affably, and she did not trouble to readjust the bedclothes so that they might cover her nudity. Instead, she spread her legs wide apart. "See, oh honorable master," she smiled, "see how beautiful it still is!"

Muro-matchi deposited the tray on a little table on the floor and advanced to The Lily.

"M-m," he said as he fingered the ruby lips, "m-m . . . yes . . . yes . . . come now. Drink this tea and then attire thyself well. I shall have a hairdresser here to arrange your coiffure in a style that now prevails and I shall have a blind masseuse bring life to your little body." He patted her buttocks and then pattered slowly away, never taking his eyes from her outstretched and nude beauty. He chuckled as he thought of the profit he was going to make from her in selling her at the *Shin-Yoshiwara*. No place but the *O-Mise*, the first-class house, should have her.

Two hours later, The Lily was ready for the procurer. Her black hair was becomingly set in a high coiffure atop her head. Long, lacquered hairpins of wood jutted out in pleasing arrangements. Her hair glittered brightly from the *bin tsuke* that had been rubbed in so as to give it a heavy black appearance and also so that it would lay where the hairdresser had arranged it. A purple, flowered kimono with an enormous *obi* around it set off the beauty that was her natural complexion. And that was where The Lily differed. Always she insisted that she would never paint herself with the liquid powder that the other *yuyo* affected. She knew that her natural complexion was beautiful enough without having to resort to unnatural artifices. Instead of her face being painted a deathly-white, it was a beautiful shell-pink color. Her eyelids, however, had been painted with a sort of grayish color that accentuated them and above her eyes there flowed the long, graceful lines of pencilled eyebrows.

As she stood in her room awaiting the entrance of *Muro-matchi*, she appeared to be like one of the Japanese dolls that one sees scattered around the Japanese home. And one could tell from the smile at the corners of her mouth that The Lily was intensely satisfied with herself and with the appearance that she was making in her finery.

Muro-matchi's first reaction was to stand open-mouthed at the doorway, when he first glimpsed her beauty. But when he saw that she had neglected to whiten her face, he was horrified and demanded that she rectify the omission immediately. But The Lily was adamant. Tearfully she refused to accede to the procurer's demands. And, no matter how he blustered and stormed around the room, she stood quietly, her hands folded in front of her, and refused to do as he demanded. When he finally saw that she was not to be moved, *Muro-matchi* gave in with a sigh and turned to the door. "Come," he said, "we are off for your next home."

And as The Lily clattered down the stairs in her *geta* after the procurer, she could not help but give a disturbed thought to the home she was now going to.

Outside of the hotel, *Muro-matchi* helped her into an ornate *jinriksha*. In the shafts The Lily saw the enormous figure of Chang, the Chinaman of the evening before. She saw that although his eyes were downcast in respect to his master, he was still stealing a glance at her. And as he bent down to take hold of the shafts, The Lily recalled her experiences of the night before when she saw the great muscles tense in his arms and his bare legs. And she sighed. She wondered whether there were going to be any more nights of a million pleasures.

Through the dark, narrow streets Chang ran with the *jinriksha* trailing behind him. Finally, after a half hour's run, The Lily began to detect a foreign odor in the air. Where there had been solely the odor of stale bodies and *daiken radish,* which one seemed to be able to smell everywhere almost, there was now mingled strong odors of the country, of things growing, of fir trees and flowers and cherry blossoms.

"Where are we going, oh honorable master?" The Lily enquired of *Muro-matchi,* who was seated next to her, his hands folded over his paunch, his eyes closed as if in sleep. In reality, he was not sleeping but he was going over the coming transactions in his head so that, when the time came for them, he would be fully prepared and he would not be caught unawares.

"Bother not thy little head over such trifles," he parried her, and once more closed his eyes, as though the one thing in the world he desired was more sleep.

The Lily was too enchanted with her new surroundings to give another thought as to her destination. Instead, she sniffed the change of odors deeply and took in the lovely countryside that was unfolding itself to her.

Mile after mile Chang traveled until they were almost an hour out of the place from which they had started. Then, just as they had reached the top of a hill, The Lily looked down into the valley and saw a great group of houses surrounded by a moat in which there was no water. At that moment, they passed a group of coolies, clad in their blue jeans and jackets. And the coolies all laughed and pointed with their fingers to the group of buildings; The Lily overheard them saying to each other, "*naka ye yuku . . . nake ye yuku.*" She did not understand what they meant but, later on, she learned that it implied that she was going inside the *Yoshiwara* . . . to stay.

The Lily nudged *Muro-matchi* and demanded an explanation of what the coolies had said. But the procurer, as though he were brushing away a droning fly, avoided her question and continued to keep his eyes closed.

Soon, they came to the moat and The Lily saw that the road on which they were traveling continued on into the enclosure of buildings under a great gate on which a number of figures had been inscribed. Atop the two pylons of each gate stood an ornamental lamp. At the left side of the gate there grew an enormous weeping willow tree, its branches bent down to the ground as though in sorrow. On the other side near the *jinja,* or shrine, stood two uniformed policemen who saluted their *jinricksha* when they passed them at the gate. A tree flowering a million white blooms decorated the street.

"What is this?" The Lily suddenly demanded of the procurer.

But still *Muro-matchi* refrained from enlightening her. Instead he looked her over entirely to see that she was as presentable as possible and directed Chang to turn at the second street, the *ageya-machi* on which his friend was located.

In a short while, the *jinriksha* drew up to an ornate, two-storied building that was the *Shingawa-ro* brothel owned and operated by one, *Sato-kin*, a kinsman of the procurer. Once inside the establishment, The Lily and the procurer were directed into the tiny room occupied by the *banto*, or head clerk.

"I would speak with your master!" *Muromatchi* demanded of the squint-eyed, owlish individual who handled the business affairs of the brothel and whose powers were almost the equal of the *kutsuwa*, or owner of the establishment.

In a moment, that individual entered noiselessly in his stockinged feet. He bowed low to the procurer who, in turn, returned the bow. Then, almost automatically, the *kutsuwa* turned to The Lily and stared intently at her.

"Let us hope," he sniffed disparagingly, "that this *yuyo* turns out more favorably than the last one." This he said so as not to show his enthusiasm, for he realized that The Lily was an exceptional item indeed.

"Does not *O Tishi San* earn her keep?" the procurer retaliated, "and more? Friends who have visited her have informed me that the *mawashi-beya* of *O Tishi San* is ever filled with prospective guests who must wait for her until she is ready for them."

The moment The Lily heard the *kutsuwa* refer to her as *yuyo*, she understood where she had been taken. She was in the *Yoshiwara*. And she did not want to be a *yuyo*. She wanted to be a *geisha* girl. She wanted to dance and sing and play the *samisen*. And, after having entertained a man with all of these accomplishments, she wanted then to have him take her and worm his thing into her so that there was no second but that it did not feel that she was in heaven.

"I do not wish to be a *yuyo!*" she screamed at the top of her voice as she ran over to *Muro-matchi* and beat her tiny fists against his chest. "I do not want to be a *yuyo! I* do not want to be a *yuyo!*"

"She has spirit!" the brothel owner murmured as he seized hold of The Lily and dragged her away from the procurer. Then he called aloud for his *yarite* who managed the girls for him. She came running out from her room at the bottom of the stairs and, taking in the situation at a glance and no doubt having had similar situations present themselves, she seized The Lily and held her in her grasp.

"Take her into your room until my honorable friend and myself have completed our business!" the *kutsuwa* commanded, and he turned to *Muro-matchi* and began to talk about everything but the purchase of The Lily. For an hour they conversed thusly over cups of sake and finally, when the procurer casually brought the conversation around to it, The Lily's purchase price was eventually decided upon.

In the *yarite's* room, The Lily had thrown herself down on the mattress bed and was weeping sad, copious tears into the quilts. The *yarite*, with the usual bland words of an *obasan*, spoke to her like a "little auntie" and advised her to accept her fate, for there was nothing that she could do to help herself. She described to Lily the beauties of the life of a *yuyo* in the *Yoshiwara* and told her of the beautiful kimono she would wear and the gorgeous articles of bed clothing that would be hers in time.

But The Lily continued to weep, unheeding the honeyed words of the *yarite*. She knew only that she did not want to be deprived of the beautiful life of a *geisha* girl. And when the brothel owner entered the room later on and saw her disarranged kimono displaying a delicious expanse of limb, he could not help bending over her and stroking the flesh.

The Lily recoiled instantly at the touch and shrank away from him to the furthest side of the bed.

"Are you afraid of *Sato-kin,* the honorable master?" he inquired softly.

"I do not want to be a *yuyo!*" The Lily wept.

"Thou shalt not be an ordinary *yuyo,*" the *kutsuwa* continued, "but thou shalt be my chief *oiran,* the first *yuyo* of my honorable house!"

But even these words did not appease The Lily. She only wept all the more and beat the quilts with her fists. The *yarite* looked over to the scowling face of her master for a sign. And her glance roamed over to a *go-down,* the closet where she kept, among other things, a thin, wicked whip that she used on recalcitrant *yuyo.*

"You have no other choice but to be my *oiran!*" the *kutsuwa* insisted firmly. "Come, and attend to thy toilet so that I might present you to the police!" And he reached over to take hold of The Lily's hand. But she shrank further away from him. He lunged forward and finally managed to grasp her wrist. But she struggled in his hold and tried to free herself. Finally, the *yarite* lent a hand and held The Lily while the *katsuwa* adjusted his rumpled clothing and his ruffled temper. At the same moment, The Lily managed to free one hand and, with a cry, drew her sharp fingernails down over the face of the owner. And each fingernail left in its swath a path that oozed tiny drops of blood.

Fire came into the owner's eyes when he took his hand away from the scratches and saw the blood on his fingers. "Give her the whip!" he commanded, and he turned around and strode angrily out of the room. Immediately after his departure, three men stepped silently in and grimly awaited the instructions of the *yarite*, who had gone over to the *go-down* and had extracted the whip from it.

Lily cowered into a corner of the room, her eyes wide with fright. Little whimpers of fear came from her mouth and she brought her arm up to her lips to stifle the groans. At a nod from the *yarite*, the three men suddenly leaped over to the poor girl, seized hold of her and threw her, stomach down, onto the bed of quilts. The *yarite* advanced to The Lily. A peculiar glint gleamed from her eyes as though she was relishing already the thing that she was about to do. Then, with a flick of the wrist, she drew the gorgeous kimono away from The Lily and displayed the cheeks of her posterior, pouting up like a pair of goddess' lips. Beneath the ivory skin could be seen tiny rivulets of purple coursing their way like miniature rivers. Then, without a word of warning, the *yarite* brought the tail of the whip down onto The Lily's ass. It brought forth from the poor girl a howl that sounded and resounded through the entire house. Again and again the seemingly demented woman brought the wicked whip down on The Lily's bare flesh. Red welts came up where the whip drew away. Globules of blood appeared like a string of crimson beads along each welt. Where there was a minute ago a calm expanse of smooth, satiny skin there was now a tortured battlefield of pain. Once, one of the men who was holding The Lily screamed out in pain as the descending whip fell onto his hand which he had shifted so that he could touch the girl's shapely buttocks. This went on for five minutes. After that period, the *yarite* stopped and bent over The Lily.

"Well, young lady, what do you say now about a *yuyo*?"

The Lily could make no reply. All she could do was weep madly into the quilts. All she knew was that she was suffering from an intense pain that seemed to sear her innermost recesses. She did not care what happened to her now. She wanted only to be left alone in her sorrow. So she refrained from answering the *yarite* who, being satisfied that she had broken the spirit of the girl, summoned the men and left the room.

But she did not reckon with The Lily. The Lily was not built of the same flimsy stuff as the ordinary *yuyo*. In her was the fire and the spirit of a born fighter, a *samurai* perhaps, who was ever ready with his fierce, two-edged sword in olden times to defend his emperor. For an hour later found her once more the raging girl that she had been before the whipping. And when the *yarite* entered the room to investigate the racket that was going on there, she discovered not a pliant little creature but an enraged demon that was tearing apart everything that her hands touched and smashing furniture and ripping down the *kakemono* that hung on the wall. And when that demon saw the *yarite* enter the room, she gave a howl of anger and leaped to the woman as though to rend her to tatters. But the *yarite* was an old one at the game. She seized The Lily and overcame her once more and threw her bodily onto the bed. Then she summonded her master, the *katsuwa*.

"What are we to do with the minx?" she demanded. "She will not be subdued."

"We must not drive out all of the fire from her," he replied craftily. "We must leave some for the trade. She must undergo the ordeal of six!" And, with these words, he clapped his hands together and summoned his squinty *banto* to him. "Call me up half a dozen *waikaimono*, lusty fellows, for the ordeal of six!"

The *banto* leered down at The Lily and left the room. To herself, The Lily wondered what torture she was to experience now. The ordeal of six. It sounded foreboding. And as she thought, she shrank further away from the conniving pair.

In a few minutes, six enormous coolies came lumbering into the room. Until they came to the door they had been jabbering, but the moment they entered the room, they were struck dumb. But all of them seemed to know the reason for their being called, for they stared around the room and their faces lighted up when they saw the figure of The Lily recoiling from them. Immediately, the brothel owner gave them the command, "Give her the ordeal of six, dogs, and give it to her well. But harm her not. The one who dares so much as scratch her will be flogged to death!" And, with these words, he seated himself on a cushion on the floor and watched the proceedings.

The biggest coolie of the lot, a towering brute who stood well over six feet, reached over and seized The Lily. Then, with one sweep, he tore the bright kimono from her body. Another one of the coolies took his cue and snatched her *koshi-maki* and *suso-yoke* loinclothes from off her, leaving her standing naked in full view of all of the occupants of the room. For a moment, she drew herself up proudly, knowing that her body was beautiful, haughty with the knowledge that hers was as beautiful a body as the *Yoshiwara* had ever seen. But when she saw the burly coolie advance insidiously toward her, his arms outstretched to her, long arms like an ape's, his gnarled fingers fanning at the air convulsively, as though they were arching for the clutch of her fair young body, then the pride and the hauteur left her little body and she sank whimpering to her knees, her face a picture of despair and horror and fright.

Suddenly, the coolie leaped for her and seized

her around the waist. Lust was scribbled over his face. The Lily struggled to free herself from his grasp, but it was all useless. It was like trying to free oneself from the coils of a cobra. Slowly he bent her backward, backwards until she was lying at full length on the bed of mattresses on the floor. His tongue was hanging out in anticipation of what was to be. And, around him, the other five coolies all ogled every one of his actions, promising themselves that they, too, would soon be fucking the beautiful girl. The owner of the brothel's face was a mask. Perhaps the only thought that occurred to him was that here was a sinful waste of six fornications. The *yarite* in her corner seemed to enjoy the cruelty, the bestiality of it all, for she wet her lips many times with her tongue, as though they were continually dry.

When the coolie thought that The Lily was in position, he wormed himself between her legs and, with his hips, managed to pry her thighs apart so that her cunt presented itself fully for the entrance of his prick. And when he did take his cock out, one could see that he had had experience in the manipulation of it. But try as he could, he could not insert his stiff penis into the girl's hole, for she struggled too much. Finally, in desperation, the *yarite* leaped over to the struggling pair and, taking hold of the coolie's enormous spear, directed its entrance into The Lily's cunt firmly and surely, like one directs the wayward prick of a stallion into a mare. Once in the resisting quim, the coolie began to work viciously, thrusting his cock into her hole in its entirety, grunting every time he sank it to the hilt, groaning every time he withdrew it almost to the tip. The Lily, instead of fighting now, realized that the big coolie finally shot his semen into her. Then, when his prick went limp, with an expert twist of her ass and her hips, she maneuvered it out of her hole and sank back onto the bed again, her long legs tightly crossed, her knees drawn up into her stomach.

For a moment, the coolie stood over her, unsure of whether he should take another jump at the wonderful woman that lay curled up so provocatively beneath him. But, when he heard the terse "next" from the *yarite*, he stumbled away from this scene, his cock still dangling between his legs like a horse that had just finished pissing.

"Do you still not want to be a *yuyo?*" the *yarite* asked.

The Lily did not answer but wept to herself.

In reply, the *yarite* motioned to the second coolie, waiting to do his task. The *yarite* motioned to the other coolies. "You two hold her arms and legs while the other two fuck her both in the asshole and in her cunt!"

In response to her request, one of the coolies laid himself down on the mattresses and awaited the actions of his compatriots. While two of them seized her arms and legs and held them firmly, spreading her legs wide apart at the same time, the fourth member withdrew his penis from his trousers and began to frig himself until it reached its maximum size. This fellow's prick, however, did not approximate

70

the other's in length. But it more than made up for this deficiency in breadth. It was almost as thick as a man's wrist. When he saw that the two had gotten a secure hold of The Lily, he directed them to lower her body so that her asshole came down squarely on the reclining coolie's already stiffened penis which was sticking up into the air like a flagpole waiting to be draped with the flag. Slowly, surely, the two coolies lowered the poor girl's body down on the enormous prick. And, holding the two cheeks of her ass, the reclining coolie directed the course of her asshole to that it settled right around his prick. Then, with a few preliminary shoves, he managed to get the head of his prick into the aperture of her asshole. As this was the first time that The Lily had taken it in that portion of her anatomy, she naturally felt pain. Muscles, unaccustomed to being stretched, pained as though they were being cut asunder. And as the coolie slowly inserted his prick deeper and deeper into her hole, she could feel it ravaging her insides as though it were tipped with a thousand red-hot spikes.

Then, to cap it all, the coolie who had been frigging himself in front of them, suddenly directed his massive prick straight at the gaping cunt that presented itself so enticingly as the two coolies drew her legs wider apart so as to afford him easier entrance. Straight and true went the coolie's prick into The Lily's hole. And as he inserted and withdrew, he attempted to tickle the tiny clitoris that sat atop of the distended lips of the girl's quim. And all the while, the other coolie was rapidly pushing his penis into The Lily's asshole until he could push it in no further.

Thus The Lily was fucked at both ends. At one end a prick of an enormous circumference stretched the sides of her vagina almost to the breaking point while, at the other end, another enormous prick was taxing the sphincter muscles of her backside to their utmost. In and out went the duo of pricks. And both coolies grunted in passion. And the saliva slobbered down from the corners of their mouths. And the two coolies who held her legs and arms stared at the proceedings and wondered when they were to get their turn. And the *yarite* eyed the rape of The Lily and leered at the girl's predicament. His face still impassive, Oriental that he was, the owner of the brothel still sat on his haunches and surveyed the scene with the placidity of a man watching a *geisha* performance.

How long this went on, she did not know. But, in a daze, The Lily recalled one coolie suddenly blowing into her ass and then, almost immediately afterward, the other coolie shot his load into her cunt. And each withdrew his penis and retreated to the door through which they exited. The two coolies who were left stood over the prostate body of the girl and looked over to the *yarite* for a word from her to go ahead with their part of the job.

"You have had the ordeal of four," the *yarite* whispered down to The Lily. "Do you desire the ordeal of six or will you consent to becoming a *yuyo?*"

The Lily, this time, did not cower as she had

done at first. She turned around and lay on her back and looked up fearlessly into the mocking eyes of the woman. "You can rend my body to shreds but you cannot break my spirit!" she said tiredly. And in the corners of her mouth there appeared that mocking, elusive smile. And her eyes flashed the hauteur, the unashamed queenliness that was to become a trademark for The Lily.

At these words, the *yarite* motioned to the remaining two coolies who, eager to be off in the saddle, leaped quickly to the girl. But before they could continue the ravishment, a word sounded through the room.

"Stop!"

The coolies stopped in their tracks. They looked questioningly at the *yarite,* their stiff pricks already jutting out ahead of them like a pair of jousting spears. The *yarite* turned to her master, the brothel owner, who had given the command. "Why, master?"

He called her to him.

"We shall send her to the *geisha school.* She shall learn all of the arts of the *geisha.* She shall learn how to entertain men not only with her body but with her mind, with her song, with her dance and with her talk. She shall become the greatest *oiran* in Tokyo. She has everything: a beautiful body, a delightfully small cunt, finely shaped breasts, passion, complexion and spirit. We shall not break her spirit. She shall become as great an *oiran* as were *Taka-o* and *Mi-ura-ya* and *Usa-gumo* and when she dies her body will be buried in the *Dotetsu* cemetery but her name will be taken by other beautiful *oiran*. We shall take her to the *geisha* school tomorrow. Prepare her for the journey back to the city and we shall travel out to the school of my cousin, *Ono Saki*, who resides in the Street of the *Geisha*."

With these words, he left the room, followed by the *yarite* and the two grumbling coolies. And in her bed, alone, The Lily wept and wept and wondered what misfortune was next to be her lot.

When she finally feel asleep, she had horrible dreams of enormous pricks poking her this way and that, prodding her hole into a shapeless mass.

But the morrow, really, was to be the first day of her happiness.

CHAPTER FIVE

And so they took The Lily to *Ono Saki's*
School of the *Geisha.*

The Lily learned a great deal with the *geisha*
girls. She remained there, in the house on the
Street of the *Geisha* for more than a year,
during which time she learned all that there
was to know in regard to *gei,* the art of dancing, playing the *samisen,* pouring the tea cere-
monial, pouring sake, and speaking wittily. In
fact, she learned everything.

For instance, she learned that the *geisha*
should never allow herself to become drunk
with sake at a party to which she had been
called to provide the entertainment. She should
accept the proffered glasses of liquor. But, as
it is her duty to wash each glass out in a

bowl before refilling it with sake for the guest, she should raise the glass to the mouth, as though she were drinking the sake, and then lower it, still filled, to the washbowl and empty its contents therein.

Too, in time, she learned how to make the squeaking noises that the *geisha* make by means of blowing and squeezing between their lower teeth the dried and salted berry of the winter-cherry from which the pulp has been deftly extracted at the stem. The *geisha* girl does this almost as much as the American girl chews her gum.

But one of the most enjoyable things she learned was the art of cunnilingus. But perhaps this Latin word is foreign to some of my readers. The explanation is very simple. The word cunny is, of course known to my honorable readers. That word lingus is merely Latin for tongue. Thus, in cunnilingus, we have tonguing of the cunny. And that, honorable readers, is just what occurred at the School of the *Geisha*. After all, when a number of girls are segregated into one house, it is only natural that they soon discover that, sometimes, men are not necessary for the consummation of sexual pleasures. It is usually the older ones who teach the younger ones.

In every *geisha* school, there are little girls who have been bought by the *geisha* master in order to be trained for the art of the *geisha*. These little girls are called *hangyoku*, because they are half-jewels. These little girls, besides learning *gei*, are also supposed to cater to the needs of the *geisha* and act as handmaidens for them. The Lily, of course, did not have to go through this period of training. Her beauty, her natural ability to learn things, made it quite evident to the master that she had only to be taught the finer things in *gei*, that she needed only a. bit of polishing.

However, I must describe to you how The Lily first came to learn of the joys of cunnilingus. It occurred shortly after her entree into the School of the *Geisha*. She had spent a hard morning in the dance room, rehearsing the *chonkina*, a dance typical of the *Nagasaki* province. In this dance, the *geisha* use their hips considerably in harmony with their arms and feet. But most of the work is done by the hips. Later, I shall describe to you a performance of the *chonkina*, for it is the most animalistic, the most sensual dance that is ever performed by the *geisha*.

For four hours The Lily had been rehearsing this dance. So that when she finally dragged herself up to her little room, she could only throw herself down on her mattress bed. The hip muscles, unaccustomed to their exertions, ached terribly. She felt as though the lower half of her body had been worked entirely loose from the upper half. She closed her eyes and tried to compose herself to sleep.

Suddenly she felt a strange desire in her. She felt; somehow, that she had to have a man to fuck her. For two months now, she had been so absorbed in her learning of *gei* that she had had no time to think of the pleasures of sex. But now, now that she felt that strange feeling of lassitude creeping over her, she felt strangely hot. She felt as though she must be fucked. Automatically, her hand went to her cunny. And she inserted her forefinger into it and diddled her clitoris a bit. Suddenly, the door of her room opened and a little *hangyoku* entered. She stood shyly and awaited The Lily's command to enter.

"What do you want?" The Lilly asked as she drew her hands shamefully from her clitoris.

"The master bade me to come to you to massage the pain away from your hips," the *hangyoku* replied.

For a moment, The Lily considered sending the little girl out. But, a sudden twinge of pain in the region of her hips reminded her of her hurts and she turned over on her side, closed her eyes and said, "All right, little flower."

For fifteen minutes, the little girl rubbed expert hands over the sore spots in The Lily's body. Around and around she rolled her body on the mattress. And, with an aromatic oil, she rubbed the muscles of her thighs and kneaded them so that, in time, most of the pain disappeared. The Lily lay with her eyes closed during all this time, and she felt the strange feeling of lassitude creep slowly through her again. But this time the feelings of sex became magnified. For there were no more feelings of pain to interfere. Now there was only a shrieking demand to be satisfied sexually. And The Lily promised herself that the moment the little girl left her room, she would continue the frigging of her clitoris.

Just as these thoughts traversed her mind,

she felt the most delicious of sensations in the region of her thighs. Immediately, she thought that she had fallen asleep during the massage and that she was now dreaming. For, wonder of all wonders, throughout every fiber, throughout every nerve in her system, she felt an exhilerated sensation creeping. It was as though she was being fucked. For the moment, she considered opening her eyes. But then she argued, if it was a dream, then the moment she opened her eyes the dream would disappear. So she allowed her eyes to remain closed while she experienced the most delightful of sensations. In time, she felt her clitoris growing harder and the nipples of her breasts became distended and grew harder until they were like little lumps sitting atop her breasts. Within her loins there came that boiling, that seething which comes with the climax of an orgasm. And at that moment she could restrain herself no longer and she opened her eyes. In front of her she saw the little girl, the *hangyoku*, lying outsprawled between her thighs, her tongue busily forking into The Lily's cunt.

So that is what it was, The Lily thought to herself. The little girl thought she saw a look of displeasure come into The Lily's face and so she started to withdraw her tongue. But, when The Lily saw this, she immediately smiled broadly and drew the little girl's head once more back between her thighs.

"You are not displeased?" the little girl asked timidly.

"No, no!" The Lily answered emphatically.

"Rather, I am pleased, for I have ached these many moons for such as what you are now affording me!" And, with these words, she drew the *hangyoku's* head closer down between her widespread thighs so that her face was now sunk deeply into The Lily's luxuriant growth of hair.

Now the tonguing of the cunt went on in earnest. Before, the little girl had gone at her work gently because she was afraid that she might awaken The Lily. But now, now there was nothing to fear. And so she edged herself up as close as she could and inserted her busy tongue into the orifice of The Lily's cunny. Deep into it she sank its tip, first skirmishing around every inch of the vaginal lips and then going in deeper into the vaginal wall and finally around the joy bottom. This she finally took into her mouth and sucked on until it grew to fully twice its size. At this point, The Lily could stand it no longer. She felt her thighs swing involuntarily back and forth as though she had a man's prick in her hole and she was attempting to help his motions. Again the boiling came into her loins. She felt as though she could withhold herself no longer. And, as the little girl's tongue still continued to ply its trade busily, The Lily suddenly felt everything in her let go in one grand excess of emotion, and she spent her inner fluids profusely over the face of the little girl.

For a while, both girls lay back and panted out their exhaustion. Once more, The Lily felt that it was good to be alive. Of what use was a man, she reasoned, if one could enjoy oneself without him. Why should she allow herself to be manhandled, if she could get a beautiful child like this *hangyoku* to tongue her and thus bring her into an orgasm?

At that moment, the door to The Lily's room opened once more and this time, The Lily's best friend among the *geishas*, O-Yuki san, entered. And when she saw the two girls lying outstretched on the mattress, she could not help giving them both a grinning smile, as if to say, "How was it, my dears?"

In fact, her first words of greeting were, "So you have discovered the charms of the *hangyoku*, O Lily?"

"*O-Yuki san*, likewise has discovered them?" The Lily asked.

O-Yuki san laughed her little infectious laugh that the men loved so. "Without the *hangyoku*, life in the School of the *Geisha* would be unbearable. But there are other things enjoyable here too, beside the *hangyoku*," she added.

"Men?" The Lily demanded frantically.

"Sometimes," *O-Yuki san* replied, "when we have a *hokan* here to teach the *geisha* his art of comic clowning, and naughty dancing, together with the other arts of the male *geisha*."

The Lily sighed. "I do so want a man, now!"

"Perhaps later on, when the *hokan* comes, we shall contrive to get him to you," *O-Yuki san* said. "But, meanwhile, you must learn the art of the *gei*, so that when you are done with your schooling, you may be able to entertain men royally, as they should be entertained. In a year you shall have all the men your little cunny desires!"

"But what am I to do meanwhile?" The Lily demanded almost tearfully, for she already felt her feelings rising in her once more. "What am I to do now that there is in me a mighty yearning for a man's cock?"

In answer to this, *O-Yuki san* replied, "I shall show you what we *geisha* do when there is no man present to satisfy us." With these words, she left the room for a moment, leaving The Lily on her mattress wondering what there was to be taught to her next in the education of a *geisha* girl.

In a moment, *O-Yuki san* returned to the room. But this time she had a peculiar contraption in her hand. It was a long, rigid pole sort of a thing that appeared to be made of rubber and had two straps dangling down from one end. The other end was rounded off. On the whole it looked like an enormous prick. In the hole, The Lily discovered that it felt like one.

"What are you going to do with that thing?" The Lily asked fearfully, for never before had she seen as enormous a thing as it was.

In answer to this query, *O-Yuki san* doffed her kimono so that she was nude and began to strap the thing on around her waist so that the rubber prick stuck out in front of her like a man's cock at full mast.

"Oh!" was all that The Lily could say, for now she saw what was going to be her lot. "You are going to be a man with me!"

"I am going to be more than a man with you," *O-Yuki san* replied, "for I shall have two little breasts for you to play with while I fuck you with this instrument of pleasure, and I shall have two little breasts of yours to play with and to suckle. Come, let us act rather than talk." And with these words she lowered herself down to the mattress bed where The Lily was reclining.

However, before inserting her prick, she began to diddle her finger in The Lily's cunny. "Diddle my button too!" she demanded of The Lily, "for I must feel this with you, too!" In response The Lily did as she was told and, as she felt *O-Yuki san's* expert fingers drawing gently on her bottom, she did likewise and inserted her finger into *O-Yuki san's* cunny and there she took hold of the button, which was much larger than her own, and she tugged gently at it. Soon she began to feel the return of her passion once more. And, at her side, she heard the panting breaths of *O-Yuki san,* and she knew that she, too, was growing passionately hot.

"Shall we use your instrument now?" The Lily demanded, for she felt an itching in her cunny, such as she felt when she desired the entrance of the male member.

"In a short while!" *O-Yuki san* replied in gasps, for her breath was now coming in short, labored sighs. "We shall hold off until just before the orgasm. Then it will feel much better." And she started to frig her girl friend all the more while she felt The Lily's fingers exploring her own cunny avidly. Finally, when she could stand the frigging no more, when she felt that the next minute would be the one in which she must spend herself richly, she got up to her knees and took the enormous rubber thing into her hands.

"Spread your legs wide now!" she warned The Lily as she inserted the tip of the fucking machine into The Lily's quivering quim that seemed to yearn mightily for the contact. The sides of the thing seemed to have been greased beforehand, for, as she leaned gently onto the end that was strapped to her, the slim, slender artificial prick slid easily into The Lily's gaping hole with a sort of sucking noise, like a foot sinking into wet sand.

Then, with the motion as of a man, she withdrew the thing almost to its tip. The Lily sighed as she felt the prick withdraw from her very innards. "In, in!" she cried, and when she felt the enormous length sink once more into the depths of her very being, she luxuriated in the overflow of sexual emotions that it brought with it. Up and back *O-Yuki san* drew the rubber prick, grunting each time she sank it to its hilt and, wheezing when she withdrew it, imitating a man in passion as best she could. And, as she did so, The Lily kept up a constant frigging of her friend's cunt, tickling her in the most sensitive of spots, the clitoris, and, occasionally, taking the nipple of the girl's breast into her mouth and sucking it gently so that it stiffened under her tongue like a stick.

Thus the two girls lay together for some time, each one's passions raised almost to the bursting point, yet each one trying to hold herself in, so that when they could keep themselves no longer they could give vent to their emotions in one grand splurge of passion. Up and back *O-Yuki san* drew and withdrew the rubber penis. And as she pushed, The Lily pushed with her ass and rotated her hips sideways and rolled her eyes and groaned as she felt the wonderful thing within her rubbing the sides of her vagina, tickling her clitoris and pushing her womb far up into her belly, it seemed. Finally, she could stand it no longer and, with a long drawn-out sigh, she allowed the dammed up forces within her to explode so that she felt as though a great castastrophe had taken place inside of her. And she felt an extreme sense of pleasure creeping over her once more.

But somehow, behind all of the pleasure, there seemed to be a certain something lacking. Despite the fact that she had been brought up to the pitch of passion, something had been lacking. And it was not until she was next fucked by a man that she realized that what it was that had been missing was the sensation that came when she felt the sperm from the male washing up against her womb's tip as it spurted recklessly out of the prick. But now, now she tried to give herself fully over to the spirit of being fucked by a woman. And, because she had stinted herself so long, because it had been so long since she had been fucked by a man, she imagined that there was nothing more that she desired. And, as she lay back on the cushion, exhausted, she felt *O-Yuki san's* body insinuate itself onto her own body. And she felt *O-Yuki san's* lips glue themselves onto her own lips. And she felt *O-Yuki san's* tongue entwine itself around her own tongue. And she felt the hair of *O-Yuki san's* pubic section rub against the hair that fringed her own cunt, for her friend had unstrapped the machine from her and had thrown herself bodily onto The Lily and, with a circular motion of her hips, was rubbing the region of her cunt mightily into the region of The Lily's cunt.

Once more, The Lily sensed her emotions rise. Once more, she felt the button of her cunny stiffen as *O-Yuki san's* nimble fingers found their way into her hole and performed their task. Then, when they had so rubbed each other's cunts for a while, *O-Yuki san* cried out, "Now we shall lick each other, O-Lily!" And, suiting the words with action, she turned herself around so that, as she lay on The Lily's belly, her head looked into the Lily's cunny while The Lily faced her hole. In the Occident this little maneuver is known as 69. But here in Japan it is little known because we, as a people, are not addicted to such supposed perversions. But the Japanese people are quick to learn, and the *geisha* learned of the trick from visiting sailors and began practicing it whenever they got together.

Thus the two girls lay together. And, as The Lily darted her tongue into the receptive quim of *O-Yuki san* she felt *O-Yuki san's* tongue exploring her own aching cunny. The sensations that it brought forth were delicious ones, for they were entirely different from anything else she had ever experienced. And, as she felt her own love button stiffen under her friend's tongue manipulations, she felt her friend's love button stiffen under her tonguings. So that, as they advanced, both of them discovered that they were experiencing exactly the same emotions and feelings at exactly the same time. And, when the time came that they could no longer withhold themselves, they each spurted each other's pearly love fluid into each other's faces. And then they rolled over and lay back on the bed. And, in a few minutes, each had fallen off into a deep slumber, so exhausted had they become from their frenzied frigging.

The next morning, when she awoke, The Lily felt an aching pain in her back and a terrific headache was pounding her forehead. But, she did not regret the events of the previous evening and many times after that, she had occasion to sleep with her friends and fellow *geisha* girls at the *geisha* school.

But The Lily was a woman. Now there are some half-women who, although they have the bodies of women, still and all do not feel or act as women should. The Lily, however, was all woman. And only because she had kept herself away from man as long as she did, did she revert to sexual intercourse with other women. But such things cannot last forever. There comes a time in the life of a real woman when she realizes that what she is doing is artificial; that the stimulation she is giving her sexual senses is only an illusion of the real stimulation; that the kisses she gives and takes from another woman are, at best, barren fruit; that the ache in her body, the pain in her groin, the desire that rends her mind into jittery tatters is too real to allay with imitations of a man. The Lily was a real woman. And she came to realize that what she wanted was a real man, not an unreal woman.

And her time came when *Zenroku*, one of the most popular *hokan* of the *Shin-Yoshiwara*, came to the School of the *Geisha* to teach the new girls the art of comic clowing and comic dancing, both of which he was master.

Zenroku was of the small, wiry type of entertainer whose facial muscles are as agile as their legs. He had but to stare at you and wink his eye and the onlooker would go into hysterics. And when he performed the far-famed *hadaka-odori* dance, in which he pranced around entirely naked and went through all of the motions of fucking together with all the other sexual acts, accompanying his actions with a running line of droll and witty conversation, he could even make a dog laugh.

And so the time came when he was to take The Lily in hand and teach her something of his marvelous art. And teach her he did, more than anything else he had ever taught anyone else. For he taught her the art of gymnastic fuck. One of the various dances that the *hokan* is supposed to perform is called the *ashi-dori*. Here he lies on his back and, with his feet stuck straight into the air, he performs a series of gymnastic manipulations with his feet that are most extraordinary to watch.

It was a variation of the *ashi-dori* that this particular *hokan* taught The Lily. He was struck with her beauty of form and color immediately upon being presented to her. In fact, he insisted that she was to be his first pupil and that he was going to teach her his art individually. The Lily, by this time, was aching for contacts with a man. She was still a student *geisha* and was therefore unable to be sent out on call to parties where her services as a musician or a dancer or merely as a bed-woman, could be used. It was for this reason that she was frantic for a man. And the *hokan* was the first man to present himself at the *geisha* school with possibilities for a good man-fucking. And when she followed him up the stairs to her room, she knew that the evening was going to be spent in more than the art of the *hokan*. There was going to be love and fucking and all else that goes with them.

Once in the room, the *hokan* insisted that The Lily divest herself entirely of all of her clothing. This did not take long, for all she did was to unwrap her *obi* and allow her kimono to drop and she was as naked as the day she was born. The *hokan* did likewise so that he, too, was completely naked. "No clothing must be in the way to hinder us," he said, tersely, in explanation, although The Lily did not really ask for an explanation. She merely knew that she was going to get what her body was aching for. And when she saw his enormous prick dangling loosely from between a great bush of hair, she could not help but keep her eyes on its immensity and compare the life that pulsated within its lines to the deadly apathy of a rubber dildo. Immediately, the *hokan* began his lessons. But in reality, to The Lily they were nothing new. For he simply took hold of her and laid her gently down onto her mattress bed. By this time, life had begun to stir in his limp prick.

"What are you going to teach me, oh honorable *hokan?*" she asked of him, a smile coming into her eyes as she noted him preparing himself for her.

"First you must learn how to accept the will of man!" the *hokan* whispered to her, and he lay down next to her and began to kiss her breasts. Then, when he felt them stiffen under his tongue, he transferred to action to the little button in her cunny. But first he marveled at the size of it as it nestled prettily in her wreath of hair. By this time, he had worked The Lily up sufficiently so that she was ready to receive him at any moment. And he also worked his own penis up to a point where its length was almost enough to frighten even the most experienced of prostitutes. Busily his tongue worked itself into her hole. And The Lily's body twitched and shook as she felt the old thrill seething within her loins. And she moaned as though in pain. And the moment she felt the tip of the *hokan's* prick touch her button, she knew that she was going to enjoy the most beautiful of sensations. Then, gradually, he worked his long penis into the twitching lips of her agitated cunny. But, instead of being satisfied merely to fuck her, he began to explain to her different movements of the hips that she could use in order to work a lagging penis up to a hard-on, and he explained to her new uses for abdominal muscles and, in fact, muscles all over her body, which she could use in an inordinate number of ways. And all of these instructions, The Lily took in calmly. And even when she felt the piling up of waves of passion in her, even when the throes of bliss overflooded into every nook of her being at the time of the orgasm, she reflected on what she had learned from the *hokan* and she decided that she was soon going to make use of her knowledge.

The *hokan* remained with her for the entire night. After that, she needed him no more, for she had learned all that he could teach her.

Thus, oh honorable reader, I have taken you with me through the education of The Lily. We have seen her in the various stages of life-absorbing sexual knowledge like an avid child who feels the faint stirrings of sex in its loins. We see her now, at the end of her student days in the *geisha* school, a young lady who knows everything that there is to know, and more than that, in the art of fucking and being fucked. She can sing, she can dance, she can make jokes, she can pour tea, she can pour sake, she can entertain a party of men excellently.

But best of all, The Lily could fuck.

In the next chapter, I start in on the life of The Lily in the *Shin-Yoshiwara*.

In the next chapter The Lily is really going to live.

So come with me, honorable friends.

CHAPTER SIX

The ways of a woman are dark, oh honorable reader.

For who can say how it was that The Lily, after objecting so strenously to becoming a *yuyo* at the *Shin-Yoshiwara*, became inducted into the fold so docilely? For she really was docile when the owner of the brothel came one sunny morning to the *geisha* house and claimed The Lily for his own.

I have often conjectured as to the reason for The Lily's change of heart. I reasoned that, perhaps, she desired contacts with men so avidly that she could never be satisfied with the few men that she might fuck as a *geisha*. For, then, most of her time would have had to be taken up with singing and dancing and pretty talk, all of which would have been climaxed with the sexual act. Thus, for her, there would have been much time wasted. In the *Yoshiwara* she would have more men than there are views of *Fujiyama*. But even this explanation is only a surmise. And I must therefore speak of her change without explaining it. Or perhaps a sufficient explanation would be that the ways of a woman are dark.

Be that as it may, the fact remains that on one bright sunny morning the *katsuwa* of the brothel where The Lily had first been taken appeared and took her immediately to the special *Yoshiwara* detail of the police department.

Strangely enough, the special bureau of prostitution is included in governmental reports as being a part of the bureau of trade. But enough of irony. Let us continue with the story of The Lily. We have followed her into the police station. Now let us go further with her into a small room on the ground floor. Here is where The Lily is to be enrolled as a *yuyo* in the *Shin-gawa-ro* brothel.

Behind a desk on a raised platform sat two police officials, both with self-satisfied smirks spread over their faces. One of them was merely an aid to the other, who was *Sado Kato*, one of the most notorious police captains in Tokyo. His eyes were of gray steel and gave no hint of what was behind them. Never did a smile break his stony features. Instead, he always glowered down upon an unfortunate victim until the poor fellow writhed merely from the scathing looks alone and finally confessed his crime. At present, because of his success in criminal fields, *Sado Kato* had been given charge of the *Yoshiwara* police detail. There was more money in it. And now he sat behind his desk, as of old, and glowered down at The Lily and *Sato-kin* as they sidled into the room and stood in front of the desk on the raised platform.

The Lily's future employer nodded to *Sado Kato* and made a deep bow to show his great respect for that venerable arm of the law. *Sado Kato* did not deign to make a similar return of respect. Instead, he stared at the picture of a girl that sidled in after the brothel owner. His deep-set eyes lost their customary steeliness. His stern mouth, which had sent a thousand criminals weeping into the jail, opened a trifle. Never before had he seen as beautiful a *yuyo* as this one was, he thought. Thousands of young girls had been brought before him to be registered in the official government books as licensed *shogi*. But not one had promised as much as did this one. The Lily, from under her downcast eyelids, noted the faint change come into the usually stern countenance of the police captain. But she demurely continued to keeep her eyes glued to the floor.

The captain suddenly caught himself. "Harrumph!" he snorted when he realized that the mask of his face had changed at the sight of The Lily, and he tried to compose his features once more into the awful mien that was his face.

"Where is the girl's sponsor?" the police captain asked.

"I am the girl's sponsor," the brothel keeper replied.

"Where is the owner of the brothel in which the girl is to become a *yuyo?*" the captain again asked, his level voice showing no sign of his suspicions or the thoughts mulling in his brain.

"I am also the owner of the brothel," that person answered with a smirk, and he gazed steadily into the steel eyes of the captain.

"You are quite a fellow, aren't you?" the captain sneered.

"I purchased the contract of this honorable young lady last year," the brothel keeper returned, "and I placed her into the *geisha* house of my honorable friend who conducts a reputable place on the Street of the *Geisha*. Now that she has learned the art of *gei*, she has expressed her desire to return to my establishment in the *Yoshiwara*." And, turning to The Lily, he asked of her, "Is it not so, oh fair one?"

The Lily did not deign to raise her eyes. She only nodded her head in response.

The brothel keeper continued: "It is for that reason that I am both sponsor and brothel keeper at the same time, honorable captain."

The captain fiddled with his brush and murmured, "Most irregular, most irregular!" Then there was a period of silence. All that could be heard was the murmur of voices of waiting prospective *yuyo* outside the thin partitions. Finally, the brothel keeper cleared his throat. And the police captain raised his eyes from the immense volume into which he had been writing some of the information that he had received about The Lily. And he saw the right eye of the brothel keeper close slowly into a suggestive wink. And, in return, he nodded his head slowly. And he dipped his brush into the ink once more and began to write again. And, after a few more questions, both the brothel keeper and The Lily were able to retire from the presence of the police captain through another sliding door. But, as The Lily turned to go, and as she stepped to the door and through it, she felt the steely gray eyes of the captain boring into her.

And she knew that she had not seen him for the last time.

Once more The Lily found herself in the brothel of *Sato-kin* in the *Yoshiwara*. But this time, there was a different Lily. This time, instead of an uncultured, untutored Lily as at first, there was now a Lily who had been taught the ways and wiles of the *geisha*. Every motion of hers as she walked was studied and seemed to fit into a smooth, rhythmic flow of movement. As her hips swayed lightly, she managed to make her breasts jostle slightly from side to side, thus indicating that those delightful orbs of unalloyed bliss were present for man's pleasure.

First she was led into the *yarite's* room in which she had been so severely whipped about a year ago. The same *yarite* was there, sneering at her from behind a supposedly welcoming smile. The *katsuwa* entered the room rubbing the palms of his hands. "Now, my little flower, what shall we name you?" he asked.

"I have been called The Lily."

"Ah, but here, it is the custom for the *yuyo* to take the name of a famous ancient *ciran* whose beauty and exploits the poets still praise. Like those of *Miyakoji* and *Taka-o* and *Mi-ura-ya.*"

The *yarite* sniffed. "It appears to me that it is the right of the owner of the dog to name it!"

The Lily turned angrily at her tormenter. "I have been called The Lily. I shall be called The Lily. And, when I am dead, then the poets and scribes shall write their poems of me and sing their songs of me and the artists shall depict my beauty on their silks and scrolls and it shall behoove other and new *yuyo* to take the name of The Lily too!"

The owner of the brothel sensed a tiff. "I will not countenance dissatisfaction among my employees!" he shouted.

The *yarite* arose from the floor and turned to the door. "Your new *yuyo* shall be difficult to handle, master, but there is always the whip," and she left the room mumbling, "always the whip!"

"It shall be as you wish," the owner whispered to The Lily, for he saw that she was trembling, like a thoroughbred horse before a race. "From now on, your name shall be The Lily, and so it shall be posted downstairs and in the *hikite-jaya*. And I shall obtain the services of *Utamaro*, who is at present one of the greatest artists in Japan, and I will commission him to paint your picture and . . . "

"He shall need no commissioning," The Lily said, her eyes half-closed as if she were contemplating the future scene. "That he can paint me, The Lily, shall be commission and compensation enough!"

The *katsuwa* nodded his head. "Come! I shall show you to your *zashiki*. It is on the second balcony, far from the cries and noises of the street. It is only the second room of my establishment. The *ciran no o zashiki*, the first room, is on the other end of the hall where my *oiran*, *Usugumo*, now dwells." Here he dropped his voice to a whisper and, close to The Lily's ear, he said, "but *Usugumo* is slipping. Already her followers have lodged complaints with the *yarite*. Who can tell? Perhaps, within the year, there shall be a new *oiran?* Perhaps her name might be *Hana San,* or *Toshi San,*" and then, after a slight pause, "or even The Lily."

As she followed the *katsuwa* up the stairs, The Lily determined that within the month, not the year, The Lily was going to be *o shoku,* the chief girl of the house. And even when the owner pushed open the door of her *zashiki*, her eyes were not directed to the inside of the room but to the end of the hallway, where there was the room of the incumbent *oiran*.

"This is no *heya-mochi*," the owner said pridefully, "no ordinary one-room affair in a low-class establishment. For here there is not only an eight-mat *zashiki* but also a *tsugi no ma* room of four mats for your own private use. And not only that but, off of this second room, there is also a third room. Only the *o shoku* should have a third room. But you shall have it, fairest Lily."

With these words, he took her hand and showed her around the apartment. The usual *tokono-ma* alcove and *chigai-dana* recess with two shelves were there. In the alcove there hung a *kakemono* of a crane by *Chosanshu*. Around it were tastefully arranged vases of flowers, the vases being made of *Kutani* porcelain. In one corner The Lily's eyes fell on a *samisen*, a *gekkin* and a *koto*. With a little move of delight, she tripped over to the instruments, picked up the *samisen* and began to play it while she hummed an accompaniment.

For a moment, the owner regarded the scene with delight. "It was not for naught that I sent you to the School of the *Geisha*," he said. "But come, I must show you more of your *zashiki* where you shall live your precious life."

On the shelves, The Lily found a wealth of knicknacks that brought smiles of delight from her. A rabbit made of imitation crystal, perched on a tiny cushion of red crepe particularly pleased her until she saw the hanging clock on the wall and the handsome mirror. All of these things she saw in the large room. In the smaller room, the *tsugi no ma*, her own private room, the first thing she saw was the shelf on which were placed the *yuyo's yagu*, or bedclothes. What attracted her eyes was its covering of bright green *furoshiki* on which

99

was dyed the ornamental figure of a *karakusa* vine and the name of the girl to whom the room had previously belonged.

"Soon thy name shall be embroidered thereon," the owner whispered when he saw the look of displeasure creep into The Lily's face. "Here, here is a beautiful set of drawers for thy private clothing," he continued, "and here is a fine, polished *naga-hibachi* on which you can boil your water for tea in this *tetsubin*, and here is the cupboard in which are all your beautiful *yo-chaki*, with which you can conduct the tea ceremony which you have no doubt learned to conduct in the *geisha* school."

The Lily nodded to this question and was about to open the door of the cupboard to display her ability, when her attention was directed by the owner to a finely carved *kyo-dai* on the floor. Immediately, she sat herself down in front of it and looked into its mirror and arranged a few stray locks of hair in her coiffure.

The owner helped The Lily to her feet again and drew her over to the third room. "Here is the room that is given only to *oiran*. But you shall be my *oiran*, soon. That is why it is yours." With these words, he opened the door and showed her a four-mat room. "This is the *myodai-beya*," he said. "Pray that it be forever filled with guests who await thy pleasures while you are taken up with another guest. Here you will place those who wait. And if they feign sleep, as though they are not particularly anxious for thy company, know that it is only *tanuki-neiri*, badger sleep, for they do not wish to appear soft and anxious for thy charms."

"I shall learn all these things and more," The Lily replied.

The owner noticed that night was already falling. "It grows dark," he said. "Come, I shall show you thy *kagumi-futon*, the mattress on which you shall sleep . . . and love," he added thoughtfully. And he took her back into the second room. There he showed her a pile of three mattresses, the border of which was made of stuff different to that of the center, making it look like a mirror in a frame. The borders, The Lily discovered, were made of black velvet and the panels were of red crepe. With her palms together in front of her bosom, her eyes agleam with pleasure, she looked down at the beautiful *futon* that was to be her own. The owner seemed to sense the question in her eyes for he said, without having been asked, "Yes, you may try its softness."

Immediately, The Lily let herself down on the *futon*. And, as it sagged with her weight, she could not help imagining that she was going to bed with her first lover. And in her mind's eye, she tried to imagine that first lover as being *Sado Kato*, the police captain who had enrolled her as a *shogi* earlier that afternoon.

"Of whom are you thinking?" the owner asked softly of her.

"Of my first lover," she replied.

"And whom do you wish him to be?"

Just as she was about to divulge his name, the *banto* came running breathlessly into the room. The owner eyed his head clerk ominously. He was not pleased at the intrusion. Already he had entertained visions of being the first one to sip the honey of The Lily. And, in his mind, he had visualized himself already fucking her, already experiencing the pleasures of blissful love, so that his penis had taken on a unusual hardness. "Why do you interrupt me?" he bellowed at the quavering menial.

"Someone there is in the *hiki-tsuke-zashiki* who asks for The Lily!"

"Does he not know that he must first apply to the *hikite-jaya* and secondly that the house is not yet officially opened for the night and thirdly that there is no *yuyo* called The Lily with us?"

"I informed the honorable gentleman of the fact," the poor clerk wailed, "but he advised me that there is such a *yuyo* here now!"

"How can he know that The Lily is here when we have not, as yet, posted her name in the *hikite-jaya* nor placed her name in the roster of *yuyo* downstairs?"

The clerk's eyes grew wider with fear now. "He knows, master," he managed to stammer out, "because he is . . . is . . . " and he seemed unable to bring out the balance of his thoughts into speech.

"Who is he who knows so much?" the *kutsuwa* thundered.

"I do!" came quietly from the vicinity of the door.

All heads turned in that direction. There stood the straight and erect figure of *Sado Kato*, the police captain. His face scowled ominously. His brow was furrowed with wrinkles of displeasure. "Since when does *Sado Kato* have to wait in the introducing room like an ordinary person?" he demanded.

The look of anger disappeared from the brothel owner's face. Instead, there came a bland, oily smirk. And he bowed his head deferentially to the floor. "The honorable police captain loses no time," he whined.

"The honorable brothel keeper's presence together with his stinking *bantu's* is undesirable at the present moment to this august police official."

For a moment, the brothel keeper wavered, uncertain as to what he should do. But, without another word, he turned around and follows his clerk out of the room. To himself, he thought philosophically, if he cannot be first then it is as good to be second.

When the captain saw that the door had been closed behind the brothel owner, he turned to The Lily on the mattress, who had taken in all of this by-play without having spoken a word. The scowl dropped from his face. He smiled down at the beautiful creature. He saw her smile back at him. Then he began to unbutton his official coat. He stopped short when he saw that The Lily had started to untie the *obi* around her waist. "Wait!" he commanded, "for I would undress you myself. I shall strip you petal by petal, such as one would do with a flower. Petal by petal I shall strip you until what is really yourself, what is really you, shall be revealed to me in all of its nascent splendor!"

"My master's tongue has been tipped with poet's gold," The Lily answered.

"As has his mistress," the police captain retorted. "The *geisha* school, it seems, has taught you how to use your tongue nobly."

"The *geisha* school has taught me to use my tongue for other things besides the utterance of mere words," The Lily answered meaningfully, and she smiled her quaint smile. And her eyes became half-closed. And she awaited the approach of *Sado Kato*.

When he was fully disrobed of all of his official accouterments and underclothing, and when he had doffed the night-kimono that he had found in the deep, lacquered tray on the lower shelf in the *chigai-dana* shelf recess, he walked over to tht mattress where The Lily was still sitting. "I await thy pleasures with great anxiety!" she whispered to him as he bent his head closer to hers.

"Arise from thy *kuton*!" *Sado Kato* pleaded, "so that I may uncover thy beauty."

The Lily arose gracefully and placed herself before him, her tiny hands placed on her hips, her whole body posed in a rhythmic line. Tremblingly, *Sado Kato* extended his hand to her *obi* and pulled hesitatingly at one end. It came out of its knot and fell to the floor, fluttering like a purple petal. Again tremblingly, he laid his hand on her kimono and drew it away from her body, drawing the sleeves out of her arms at the same time. This too dropped to the floor in a colorful heap at her feet. Piece by piece, her varied articles of underclothing fell away from her and piled up at her feet. Finally, when the last piece had fallen away, she stood out in the twilight of the room like a glowing statue of alabaster recently emerged from the cunning fingers of a master sculptor. *Sado Kato's* eyes became wider with passion. And his breath came in short, labored gasps. And he could not help stretching out his arm and touching her thigh with his trembling fingers, as though he doubted the existence of the beautiful vision before him and had to reassure himself of her reality by touching the living flesh. Instantly, the moment his finger came into contact with her, an electrical current seemed to shoot between them. Not a word was spoken. *Sado Kato* simply lunged forward and threw his arms around the legs of the apparition that stood mockingly in front of him. In his face, he felt the soft hair of her cunny, tickling his skin like an eiderdown cushion. And in his nostrils, he sniffed the pungent odor of love that issued forth from her tiny quim. All about her now he seemed to smell this same odor of love, almost like the odor of spilled semen, but still not that. Caught in the throes of this powerful passion, the tough police captain became a child with the girl. Words were lost to him. He was struck speechless. Thoughts refused to enter his mind. His brain was a void. He could do nothing but feel. He could do nothing but feel the emotions and passions that this young girl stimulated in him. And as he groveled at her feet and moaned in despair and eyed her beauties with great, popped orbs, The Lily stood above him, the odd smile having come onto her mouth, the haunting, level stare having come into her eyes, and she wondered what had happened to the stern *Sado Kato* that had once been a police captain.

But this reaction in the man was only momentary. It was the first impression that wreaked such havoc with him. For, immediately after that, he seemed to regain his senses, for he swept The Lily off of her feet and half-ran, half-fell onto the mattresses close by. Then and there did The Lily have the first opportunity to practice what she had learned at the *geisha* school both from her sister *geishas* and from the *hokan, Zenroku.* There was no hesitation now in her response to *Sado Kato.* Confidently, surely, her little fingers went to the captain's already stiffened penis. Again the contact seemed to send an electric current through him, for his prick took a leap of at least two inches that made its skin stretch almost to its utmost. Then she spread her legs as wide as she could get them so as to allow her lover an easy entrance into her cunt which, by this time, was pulsing wildly, like a rabbit's heart.

The Lily was caught in the throes of an intense passion. With only the exception of the male *geisha,* the *hokan Zenroku,* she had not been fucked by a man for a whole year. For one whole year she had tried to satisfy her normal cravings for a man with the abnormal and totally inadequate substitution of a woman. Here, she knew, was a real live man between her legs, his stiff prick all ready to be inserted into her aching cunny, his busy hands already fumbling for her twitching clitoris and the rapidly stiffening nipples of her breasts. Eagerly, her hands went to the great prick. Slowly, as though in the rites of a ceremony, she brought the swollen thing down to the twitching lips of her cunt. A great suction seemed to have been created there at that moment for, like a boat sucked into the vortex of a whirlpool, so was the prick of *Sado Kato* sucked into the anxiously awaiting hole of The Lily. As the prick sank deeper and deeper into her innards, The Lily gave out a sigh, a great sigh of mingled pain and pleasure and passion. And she seized *Sado Kato* around the middle of his body and squeezed as hard as she could. And, as *Sado Kato's* head came down and his face came closer to hers, and his lips touched her lips, she opened her mouth slightly so that his lips fell into her lips, and through the opening of his teeth she sent her nimble tongue into his mouth, entwining itself around his tongue, exploring every cavern, every nook of his mouth until their mouths became as fused as one mouth. And, all the while, without knowing that he was doing it, without being conscious of the fact that the slowly withdrawing and reinserting the awful length of his penis into The Lily's cunt. Back and forth he sent his prick, back and forth, until The Lily imagined that she could stand it no longer. For, deep within the very bowels of her body, she felt the quiet insistence of a boiling. And the boiling became more apparent until it took on the semblance of a veritable maelstrom. And The Lily knew that soon, soon she was to feel the hot fluid come spurting from the prick of *Sado Kato*. And she tried to hold herself back so that her own fluid could be ejaculated at the same time and thus heighten the resultant pleasure. But the more she held herself back, the greater grew her alarm that she could hold herself no longer. And she moaned in terror for fear that she was not giving her lover the utmost that was in her. And, out of fear, the heretofore unused muscles in her cunny that had given her first lovers so much pleasure, the muscles of milking, they suddenly found their lost power. And, immediately, they began to function. The police captain, fully satisfied that he was still able to withhold himself from ejaculating his sperm a while longer, felt the strange insistence of those milking muscles. The same little hands that the other's had felt to be milking them now stroked the sides of his penis in The Lily's cunny. And he knew that he could hold himself no longer, for there was now a boiling in his loins. And, with a sigh, he felt something within him give way. And he knew that he had come into The Lily's cunt. And immediately afterwards, he felt an extraordinarily warm sensation there. And he knew that The Lily, too, had come with him.

The Lily, lying back now on the cushions, felt the rush of semen spouting against her womb. And the moment she did so, she herself gave way. She felt as though her bottom had dropped away from her and the tears came into her eyes. But when she realized that *Sado Kato's* face was smiling above her, when she realized that she had given him as great a pleasure as she had received from him, then she drew his head down close to hers and, with a simple kiss, sealed the bond of their amorous friendship.

Thus it was that The Lily was first fucked in the *Yoshiwara*.

Thus it was that The Lily started on her journey of passion.

Thus it was that The Lily started the myth of The Lily.

CHAPTER 7

No man ever came into contact with The Lily who did not feel the desire to have intercourse with her. Old and young, no matter what their station in life was, the mere sight of her shapely form, her ambient eyes, her succulent lips, everything that went to make up The Lily sent thrills of emotion through them.

For instance, there was the doctor who examined her at the *kubai-in Yoshiwara* infirmary. The law demands that every *yuyo*, before entering the *Yoshiwara*, must be examined for venereal diseases. In addition, once a week, she must hie herself to this hospital which is located in the northernmost corner of the *Shin-Yoshiwara* environs, close by the Inspection Office, and there be further examined to see whether she has contracted a dread disease the week previous.

As there are about three thousand *yuyo* who practice the art of fucking in the *Yoshiwara*, it stands to reason that the examining doctor must, of necessity, have become innured to the sight of a woman's body and the intimate portions of her anatomy, just as he has become calloused to death. To him, a woman's body is merely another walking hulk of flesh shaped into a woman's form.

But Dr. *Mori Doi*, who was the surgeon in charge of venereal inspection, had to reckon with more than he was accustomed to when The Lily was brought to him the morning after her arrival into the *Yoshiwara*. The first thing that he did, which surprised the interns in attendance, was to clear the examining room entirely of all other *yuyo* to be examined. "No more examinations today," he said sharply, with the intonations of one who is accustomed to having his orders followed explicitly. Then, without another word, he summarily dismissed both the interns and the nurses from the examination room. "Come back tomorrow!" he insisted, his eyes gleaming behind his shell-rimmed glasses like a young boy who is witnessing his first naked woman. He could not take his eyes off The Lily, who had seated herself demurely on a chair and was quietly awaiting her turn to be examined. Outwardly, she appeared to be demure and unconscious of her surroundings. But, had you known The Lily, you could have seen that her half-closed somnolent eyes had taken in everything and she realized fully the havoc she was creating within the doctor and the perturbation that she had caused in him.

The doctor advanced slowly to her, after he had succeeded in emptying the room of everyone else but themselves. "Who are you?" he asked slowly of her.

"I am The Lily," she answered slowly.

"You are new to the *Yoshiwara*, eh?"

The Lily nodded her head.

"And you realize why you are here?"

Again The Lily nodded her head.

"Then take off all your clothing so that I shall be able to examine you more thoroughly," the doctor continued while he seated himself in his office chair and leaned back and watched the disrobing process with an avidity that scarcely became a man of medicine. And, as the articles of clothing came off and The Lily's beauties began to become more than evident, the doctor uttered occasional "Mmms" until, when she was completely naked in front of him, Doctor *Doi* could not help but change his dubious "Mm" to an emphatic, "Ah!"

"What must I do now, honorable doctor?" The Lily asked archly, for she realized fully what her duties were going to be. Besides, the suspicious bulge that projected itself underneath the doctor's white apron in the vicinity of his penis, implied that the doctor's professional feelings had given way to his personal reactions. And, instead of a cold and calculating doctor sitting in front of The Lily, there was now a live man.

112

For a whole minute the doctor stared at the ravishing flower that had unfolded and unpetalled itself in front of him. Then, suddenly, he caught himself and directed The Lily over to a white operating table in the center of the room. "Lie down there!" he commanded slowly, mulling over in his head what procedure he would take next.

The Lily did as she was bade. It was not unpleasant to do as you were bade, providing the one who commanded you was young and was so obviously a man. The evening before had been spent in a riotous confusion of love and passionate embraces with *Sado Kato*, the police captain. There was no reason why she should not spend the morning after similarly, with the honorable Doctor *Mori Doi*. And, without being told what to do, she spread her legs wide on the operating table and lay back with her eyes closed, as though she were expecting the onslaughts of a lover instead of the inspection of a doctor.

But she was not surprised when she realized, in a moment, that she was going to experience the former instead of the latter. For, lo and behold, when she opened her eyes again, she saw that the doctor had hastily doffed his white apron and trousers and was standing there in front of her, menacing her with an enlarged penis which seemed to sense no professional hesitancy.

"How about the honorable examination, honorable doctor?" The Lily inquired.

"Here is as good a tool as any to examine as delicious a cunny as you have!" the doctor replied, shaking the object in question vigorously in front of him. "With this tool I shall examine you minutely!" Without another word, he crawled up onto the narrow operating table and laid himself directly on top of The Lily. To herself, The Lily thought: "Am I being examined to determine my health or to determine the wealth of my knowledge in the varied arts of fornication?"

But there was no doubt in her mind when she felt the doctor insert a decidedly stiff tool into her cunt, then manipulate it in as expert a manner as she could desire. She did not lose a moment in reciprocating the doctor's motions. But, to add to it, she recalled the teachings of the *hokan Zenroku* and began a series of circular movements with her ass, punctuating them at times with a severe thrust forward to augment further the thrusts from the doctor's stiff prick. Back and forward both of their bodies went. And as they moved, the springs in the table creaked and made a sort of diabolical accompaniment to their frenzied fucking.

"Am I acceptable?" The Lilly managed to murmur despite her heated panting.

"In more ways than one!" the doctor replied, and to emphasize his remarks, he gave an additional thrust with his penis that sent it whamming, charging deep into the hitherto untouched portions of The Lily's quim. The pleasure that this unexpected movement afforded her was indescribable. And, to repay the doctor, she decided to give him a taste of her specialty, the milking muscles. And so, calculating the exact time for this nicety, the moment he had thrust his prick deeply into her hole and just before he was about to withdraw it again, she directed her cunt muscles to contract slightly so that, as the doctor's penis was slowly withdrawn by him, he felt the grasp of tiny hands on its entirety, gently tugging at its length, but firmly sucking and milking him. The sensation was both surprising and delightful at the same time. And after he had withdrawn almost entirely, the doctor looked down at his prick to see just what had happened to it. But there was nothing wrong with it. It was still rigid and dewy with the pearly essences from The Lily's vaginal discharges of lubricating fluids. Then the doctor looked down into the eyes of The Lily under him, as if to say, "Was that you?" The Lily understood his unspoken question and smiled. "Do you like it?" she asked.

The doctor was almost stunned. "Like it?" he asked, and he dropped his lips to The Lily's and kissed her again and again on her mouth and on her eyes and in the hollows of her throat in abject thankfulness for the supreme pleasure that she had given him. "What magic has the little flower learned from the *geisha* masters that she can manipulate her vaginal muscles so well?"

Again The Lily smiled enigmatically and shrugged her shoulders diffidently. "What matters where I have learned the art, honorable doctor, so long as I have learned it? Be satisfied that I may practice it on you." And, with a little moan, she threw her entire lower torso forward with a quick wrench so that his partially withdrawn prick sank deeper into her cleft. "Time flies and the hours and minutes and seconds are made for a million pleasures!" she concluded.

For the rest of the afternoon, they made the most of time.

Time and again, the doctor was made to revel in the orgies and bliss that flowed over him whenever the Lily manipulated her strange muscles of pleasure. And he decided that when their pleasures were over and after they had rested somewhat from their labors, he must devote some time to examining her vagina to determine, if only for scientific reasons, the source of The Lily's marvelous gift. And so, after the last fuck was over, and after they had rested a few moments from the exertions of the past few hours, Doctor *Doi* turned to The Lily and opened her thighs as wide as he could possibly get them. Then, adjusting an operating lamp so that the powerful rays were reflected directly on her cunny, he separated first the two little lips that guarded the portal to The Lily's once-treasured virgin gold. Directly inside of these lips, he saw another pair of fleshy lips, quivering and trembling, both from the actions of the past and from the contact of the doctor's fingers. Wide open the doctor spread these last two lips so that, with the aid of the lamp, he was able to view the entire vaginal orifice.

"Is . . . is there something wrong?" The Lily gasped frightenedly.

The doctor did not reply. Instead, he searched diligently over the entire inner surface of the quim touching this projection and that, testing this muscle and that and occasionally emitting a serious, "Mm!"

Again The Lily demanded in perturbation, "Is there something wrong with me, honorable doctor?"

The doctor's face broke out into smiles. "Wrong? Little Flower, there is everything right with you. For you have been gifted with as powerfully developed a set of sphincter of the vagina muscles together with the levator ani muscles as I have ever seen in my entire medical career!" and, as an afterthought he added, "or experienced."

The Lily was still nonplussed. The medical expressions meant only one thing to her, disease. "But am I not to come into the *Yoshiwara* because of it?" she asked, and a tear teetered perilously on her eyelids.

"My dear Lily!" the doctor beamed, "with your beauty, with your mind, with this precious gift that you own in your delicious little cunny, you shall never be able to leave the *Yoshiwara*. For your guests shall number in the thousands. Your name shall be enshrined by the poets of the land as a paragon of beauty and as an expert in the Art of a Thousand Pleasures!"

The Lily's eyes brightened at these words. The smile that came into them twinkled all the more behind the pearls of tears that had come into them. She lay back on the operating table, her arms thrown back and folded under her head. And she ruminated on what the doctor had said.

She knew that it was good to be alive.

Outside, the *bantu* awaited The Lily's exit

so that he could accompany her back to the brothel of his master. Clerks are clerks the world over. In America, all clerks look as if they punch time clocks incessantly. Here in Japan, the clerks look as though they are being continually punched by their employers. They are a spineless, weak-minded, vacillating class of people whose initiative to dare, to strive, to accomplish something creative is nil. That is why the *bantu* of The Lily's establishment, one *Ito Shin*, remained outside of the infirmary and awaited The Lily. His weak eyes, rheumy behind his heavy, shell-rimmed glasses, were amply indicative of the fish in his ancestry.

Yesterday he had been satisfied to remain a *bantu*. Today, because something had come into his life, strange feelings of resentment had crept into his mind. The something was The Lily. Yes, the insignificant *bantu, Ito Shin,* had fallen in love with that vision of loveliness, The Lily. But, because of her loveliness, she was all the more beyond his most fantastic expectations. He would have cut himself into a hundred pieces, were The Lily to have commanded him to do so.

Outside the infirmary, he commanded the *jinriksha* boy to polish his vehicle and, like a typical menial who has been accorded an iota of power, he tongue-lashed the two *wakaimono* who had accompanied them on their trip from the brothel to the infirmary. And the longer The Lily remained with the doctor, the more wrathful did the *bantu* become. For he realized the sort of examination that she was undergoing. He knew that somewhere in the hospital,

The Lily was being fucked and fucked by the good-looking Doctor *Moi*. And the *bantu* cursed the doctor for being so well built. And he cursed himself for being so ugly and spineless. He cursed The Lily for allowing the doctor to do with her as he desired. But the moment he cursed The Lily he stopped short, as though he had bitten his tongue. And, as an ameliorant to his anger, he kicked one of the *wakaimono* viciously for daring to seat himself in the shade and rest.

Finally, The Lily emerged from the infirmary. Her face gave no sign as to what had gone on behind the closed doors. Demurely she waited at the entrance for the *jinriksha* boy to draw his cart up to her. The *bantu* fawned at her side and eyed her lips incessantly, determined that no word of hers would miss his ears. Finally, unable to control his curiosity, he asked, "And did the honorable doctor find The Lily acceptable to the *Yoshiwara?*"

The Lily looked down contemptuously at the figure at her side. "Were you to be other than a fool, honorable *bantu,* you would know that The Lily is acceptable to all men!" When she saw the poor *bantu* accept this reproof as though he had received a blow on the cheek, she added more out of pity than of sympathy, "even to a *bantu!*"

The *bantu's* face lit up again. And when The Lily gave him her little hand so that he could help her into the *jinriksha,* the little man almost swooned with joy so that he forgot to admonish the young fellows who jogged along behind them as the *jinriksha* pulled away from the infirmary to travel down *Suido-jiri* street. Even as they crossed the moat that surrounded the *Yoshiwara* and passed *Kyo-machi* street, the *bantu* remained in a daze, holding onto the spot in his hand that The Lily had inadvertently touched, as though it might disappear were he to take his hand away.

Turning down *Ageya-machi* street, they finally reached their establishment. Again The Lily gave her hand to the *bantu*. And, again his joy reached such bounds that he neglected to give the *wakaimono* or the *jinriksha* boy his customary kick of parting. Instead, he stared at the back of his divinity as she minced into the brothel. After a moment, he followed her in.

Only the *yarite* was there to greet them. She did not deign to notice the presence of The Lily. Instead, she snubbed her completely by walking past her and engaging the *bantu* in conversation. "What horrid diseases has the wench got?" she demanded imperiously of the *bantu*.

The Lily did not allow this slight to ruffle her calm. She merely continued past the *yarite* until she reached the uppermost step of the stairs. Then she turned around. "Will you please to see me in my *zashiki*, honorable *Ito Shin?*" With these words, she turned again and continued to her room.

The *bantu* leaped away from his talk with the *yarite* as though a powerful electric magnet had been directed at him from the top of the stairs.

"Wait!" the *yarite* commanded.

But *Ito Shin* was already too far beyond her

call to hear what she wanted. Only one thing beat on his brain. The Lily had invited him into her *zashiki*. And as he took the steps four at a time, he tried to visualize the reception that he would get from The Lily when he did enter her room.

Hesitatingly, his every nerve tingling from suppressed excitement, the poor love-stricken *bantu* pushed the door open. For the moment he could not summon up enough courage to force himself to desecrate the sanctity of her room by entering it. And only when The Lily, from her reclining position on her *kuton* bed of mattresses, signaled him, did he step into the room. For the first time now, he was all alone with this dream of fair women. For the first time there was nobody with him to keep him from attempting that which had occupied his dreams both night and day. But the poor fool did nothing. The poor fool did nothing that he had promised himself he would do. He merely stood first on one leg and then on the other, his hands folded in front of him, his cheeks inflamed from embarrassment.

The Lily shifted her right leg across her left and allowed the front of her kimono to drop down, displaying her shapely leg practically to the shadowed niche of her cleft. The poor fellow's eyes dropped to the leg and stayed there. His eyes seemed to grow wider. "Why do you stand there gawking like a fool?" The Lily asked impatiently.

The *bantu* could not speak a word.

"Come closer to me!" she demanded.

He did as he was bade, like a sheep.

Now he stood almost at her side. Still he said nothing.

"Why don't you say something, fool?" she continued.

Still he remained silent.

"What is that enormous hump growing between your legs?" she suddenly demanded of him. And, without another word, she pushed aside the flap of his gown and inserted her hand into it. Immediately, she withdrew an enormous prick, so large as to be almost out of proportion to the size of the man, who sported it.

"Oh ho!" The Lily laughed, as she diddled it with her hand and weighed its heft speculatively, as though she were attempting to determine how it would fit into her own tiny receptacle for such things, "what have we here?"

The poor *bantu* became even more embarrassed. Almost apologetically, he said, "I am sorry for its size. But . . . but . . . I was born with it. I . . ."

The Lily laughed uproariously into his face. "Why do you speak so apologetically when you should be proud of such a possession?"

The *bantu* dropped his eyes to the floor. "Would that my wife thought as you do. For she abhors its size and vows she will divorce me for it. And I must needs go without her night after night because of it!"

This brought another outburst of laughter from The Lily. "Man!" she said wildly, "let me see how you make use of that which Buddha has so bountifully blessed you with!" And with these words she lifted the huge hulk in both of her hands and brought its tip to her mouth.

The moment the tip of her tongue touched the point of the gigantic juggernaut of a jigger, it seemed to take a sudden spurt of a few inches. It was all she could do merely to insert the head of the prick into her mouth. But to compensate for this, she dug deeper into his gown and withdrew his balls. Truly, they did justice to the prick they served. The Lily gave a moue of delight when she caught sight of their marvelous proportion. "Tell thy wife she is a fool, an arrant fool!" she laughed, as she inserted his prick once more into her mouth, that is, as much of it as she could insert, and began to tickle his hairy balls with her fingers.

It did not require very much time for the *bantu's* prick to distend itself to its real size. Mere words alone cannot describe the awful proportions of the rampaging cock. Throughout its entire length, tiny purple rivulets of veins could be seen carrying the ichor, the blood from which this truly great machine derived its strength and size. And, in the same rhythm as the heartbeat, it seemed to pulsate like a live thing. What would a French roue or a Spanish rake or an English Don Juan have given to possess so magnificent a love tool? Surely, Buddha, with all his wisdom, erred when he bestowed this inconsequential *Samurai* with so powerful a sword. *Ito Shin,* thin, stoop-shouldered, begoggled with horrid shell-rimmed glasses, nearsighted almost, hardly what one could term a lover of lovers, yet graced with a prick that should have been doing yeoman duty for a profligate nobleman. Nature is sometimes capable of perpetrating the most peculiar of monstrosities, the most hideous of jokes.

But enough of these words of envy on the part of your humble scrivener. Let us immediately repair to the jousting field where we are to witness the bout between this redoubtable lance and The Lily, in mortal combat.

There the *bantu* stood, his legs spread apart, his prick standing out from his body like a flagpole from a building. But he did not seem able to know what his next step would be. He stood next to The Lily, his mouth open, his eyes still popping like a scared child, his hands dangling at his sides. "What are you going to do with that thing now that you have brought it up?" The Lily asked of him.

The *bantu* shook his head from side to side.

Still laughing gaily, The Lily impatiently took him by the arm and drew him down to her pile of mattresses, where he knelt down in front of her and awaited her next move which was to divest herself of all of her clothing. This appalled the *bantu* even more. For never before had he seen so beautiful, so marvelously shaped a body. His wife, typical of all Japanese women, was short and frumpy looking. And her bones jutted out from the most unexpected places. And there was an ugly patch of hair under her arms and over her legs and arms and in her cleft. And she smelled like a dead cat. But here in front of him, for his own delectation, there lay the figure of a woman of whom one only dared to dream. And from her there came an odor that was as a thousand flowers combined. And between her legs, instead of a flabby, discolored pair of vaginal lips, there was a rosy-hued, pouting pair of lips that twinkled invitingly for him to enter.

Still he did not know what to do next.

And so The Lily, taking his great tool into her hand again, tugged slightly at it so that he was forced to move closer to her on his knees so that he now knelt directly between her thighs. Directly in front of his cock, the dewy hole of The Lily pulsed for the contact of him. Slowly, surely, The Lily directed the perfect penis into the paradise that was her cunny. The moment he felt the tiny lips separate to allow him entrance, he seemed to recoil slightly so that his prick slipped from The Lily's hand. But she grabbed quickly for it and again inserted it into her cunt, this time holding it firmly and directing its course perfectly so that it grooved itself into her without a stop, first grazing her already stiffened clitoris and then continuing on into her quim proper. But suddenly, he could shove no further. The size of her hole seemed to impede the progress of his prick. And, as the innate man in him directed his movements, he started once more to lean heavily against his inserted prick. This time The Lily emitted a moan of pain. She felt as though a thousand poles were being plugged into her bottom. But she had looked forward so much to the pleasure of this fuck. She could not resist the awful pokings of this magnificent mountain of a cock. She must stand the man. She must try to push the pain back, back into her consciousness and bring the sexual pleasure to the fore so that the pain would be forgotten in the overflow of passion. And so, biting her lips, she nodded to the frightened *bantu,* who was on the verge of withdrawing his prick and go slinking out like a whipped cur. "Go further . . . further!" she commanded between her withheld grunts of pain. "I must feel you all the way in me, even though it kills me!"

The *bantu* refused to move now, so frightened was he at her distress. The Lily, losing her self-control, began to weep and beat him on his chest with her tiny fists. "Have me, have me!" she wept. "Lean hard on thy staff!"

But he still could not be gotten to move.

In desperation, The Lily decided to go through the movements herself. So, steeling herself to the pain, she thrust her ass forward with a jerk that sent almost half of the *bantu's* prick into her cunt. The pleasure was indescribable for her. Whatever pain that she experienced was pushed into the background. She felt only an inexpressible, ineffable sensation now. And, to heighten it all the more, she began to manipulate her body, introducing the various twists and turns that the *hokan Zenroku* had taught her, impaling herself on the stiff rod of the stricken *bantu* like an insect specimen on a pin, drawing her buttocks and hips and, in fact, her whole body up and back, up and back, each time allowing the enormous thing to sink deeper into her, until she suddenly felt the tip of his prick graze the most indrawn portion of her womb. At this point, she was unable to continue any further with her frenzied attempts at fucking herself with the *bantu's* prick. With a deepseated moan, she fell back on the cushions, panting from passion and her strenuous efforts, her whole body quivering from excitement and the after-effects of hard labor.

Then it was that the spark of manhood blazed up in the prick of the *bantu*. The same contact that sent The Lily back to the cushions, panting from physical exhaustion, now did exactly the opposite to the, heretofore rigid *bantu*. It electrified him into action. The moment he felt the tip of his prick graze the projection in her cunny, he seemed to realize that he was fucking one of the most beautiful women in the Japanese Empire. The dormant emotions within him threw off their sleep-ridden chains. His prick took a sudden spurt forward like a race-horse at the rise of the barrier. In, in, deep into her he sank his shaft of pleasure, straining her quim to its utmost, rubbing the sides of her cunny with such a lascivious friction that she was forced to suck her guts into her stomach in order to allay the intense pain of pleasure that gripped her so suddenly. Something akin to a frenzy seemed to have seized the once inept *bantu*. For, with a vigor that verged on madness, he continued to insert and withdraw his still stiffened penis like a man gone berserk.

It was necessary now for The Lily to practice her art of milking. There was too much prick in her. She could only lay back against the cushions and allow the monster of a prick to ravage her so deliciously. Like a faint echo in a dark night, she sensed the suggestion of an orgasm creeping up on her. Deep within her loins, like a hidden spring of water a thousand miles in the bowels of Mother Earth, she felt

127

the bubbling of her own spring. And she tried to hold it back. But her passion was too great. And she felt it grow greater and greater by leaps and bounds. And before she knew it, she felt everything within her give way to the unstoppable onslaughts of the orgasm. She felt herself flooded with a refulgent glow of happiness. And at the same moment she felt the spur of semen within her cunt from the charging prick. The overwhelming bliss was increased even a hundredfold, and she wrapped her legs around the recumbent body of the *bantu*, as he lay panting on her belly, so as to keep his precious possession in her as long as possible. She felt it grow smaller and smaller in her. She dropped her lips to the *bantu's* lips and kissed him wildly. And as the juices from their mouths mingled so did the love juices from their sexual organs mingle. So that they were made to feel as one person. So that they were made to feel that nothing but they, themselves, existed in the world.

So that they were made to feel that nothing else but love matters in this world.

Truly, The Lily was on her way to immortality.

CHAPTER 8

These were the experiences of The Lily during her first night as a *yuyo* in the brothel of the *Shin-Yoshiwara*.

Her name, together with a photograph, had been filed in its proper order in all of the seven *hikite-jaya* within the *kuruwa* enclosure. Of course, there were more than seven *hikite-jaya*, but these seven were the first-class ones and sent only a high grade of clientele to the brothel in which The Lily was now awaiting the call of her first visitor.

But first, perhaps it would be best if I were to explain just what the Japanese *hikite-jaya* is. In America (in most Occidental countries for that matter), one merely goes into the whorehouse and chooses his companion for the night from the dozen or so prostitutes who parade their charms in front of him in all stages of deshabille. But here, in Japan, we go about such matters in a more refined way. The business of the *hikite-jaya* is to act as a guide to the various brothels, between the guests and the courtesans. The reception of guests and arrangement of affairs for them is attended to by servant maids, three or four of whom are generally employed in each *hikite-jaya*. The literal meaning of *hikite-jaya* is "leading-by-the-hand-teahouses." But, in reality, there is no tea sold at the place. Among the *nana-fushigi* or "the seven mysteries" of the *Yoshiwara* is made the statement, "though the introducing houses are called *chaya*, teahouses, yet they sell no tea." Another humorous mystery to the prostitutes is that "although the old women in the brothels are called *yarite*, givers, they really give nothing but trouble and take all they can get." But to the *hikite-jaya*.

When a visitor arrives in front of the entrance of a *hikite-jaya*, the mistress of the house and her maid-servants run to welcome him with cries of *"Irrasshai*, you are very welcome!" On entering the room to which he is conducted, if he is a stranger, the attendant asks him the name of the particular brothel to which he desires to go as well as the name of the young lady whose company he is desirous of having for the night. If he has no specific choice in the matter, an album of photographs is submitted to him and, from it, he chooses she who is to grace his bed that evening. This accomplished, the attendant guides the guest to his selected brothel, acts as a go-between in negotiating for the courtesan's favors and, after all the preliminaries have been settled, will wait diligently upon the guest throughout the banquet which invariably follows, taking care to keep the sake bottles moving and the cups replenished. By and by, when the time comes for retiring, the attendant conducts the guest to his sleeping apartment, waits until the arrival of the *yuyo* and then slips discreetly away and leaves the brothel. When one of these servant maids takes charge of a visitor she becomes, for the time being, the actual personal servant of the guest and attends to everything he desires. To perform the services rendered by her is professionally spoken as *mawasu,* or to move around, because she goes bustling around in order to arrange a hundred and one matters for the guest for whom she is in attendance. If he calls for *geisha,* the maid carries the *geisha's samisen* and the guest's nightgown in the left hand and a *kamban chochin,* a lantern, and a white porcelain sake bottle in the right.

The payment of the guest's bill is made through the *hikite-jaya* on his return to the introducing house in the morning. He pays his total bill to the *hikite-jaya* and the latter squares up accounts with the brothel.

That is one way in which a guest obtains the services of a *yuyo.* Nowadays, in the *Yoshiwara,* the system has been somewhat simplified in that the guest goes directly to the brothel and there chooses from the photographs the girl whom he desires. However, in The Lily's day, such was not the case. Either one went to the *hikite-jaya* where one was introduced to the brothel, or one went directly to the brothel itself where, behind the bars of outside cages, one saw the lineup of *yuyo* which that particular brothel housed. There you made your choice and, upon entering, you went up to the room of the young lady and awaited her arrival. Only in the first-class houses was this practice abolished. But The Lily, as yet, was not in the first house. That is why, during the first week of her stay at the brothel, she was forced to undergo the same humiliation as did the other *yuyo* in being displayed in the outer cages like veritable animals.

During her first evening at the brothel, she often recalled that, strangely enough, when the deep-toned curfew bell of the *Iriya* sent forth its resonant and melancholy clang reverberation over the hills and dales from its templed habitat, then was the time she was told that she had to troop down to the cages with the other *yuyo* and display her charms for the benefit of a possible guest. Then was the time that the *yuyo* struck a bundle of wooden clogshecks, *gesoku-fuda*, against the floor and, while slapping the squeaking pillar of the entrance door with the palm of her hand, imitated the squeaking of a rat.

Jostled by the other *yuyo*, The Lily filed down the stairs and into the cages where, seated in a double row, they adjusted themselves comfortably, primped a few stray hairs of their coiffures into place, and patiently awaited a call from the *bantu* informing them that their services were required inside. Twilight was just falling. The flowers of the *Yoshiwara* were beginning to bud and blossom.

The Lily looked contemptuously around her. All this, she knew, was below her. She would countenance it for only so long. Then, when she had learned what there was to learn, she would insist on her independence. From the corner of her eye, she saw that the *oiran*, the chief whore, was likewise looking at her through the corner of her eye. She was sizing the new girl up. Rumor had it that The Lily was the choice of the owner to replace her. And so she adjusted the coral and tortoise-shell hairpins stuck around her head like a saint's glory, adjusted the folds of her heavy gold and silk embroidered kimono, and fluffed out the wings of her flowered *obi*. She was indeed, an *o shoku kabu*, this proud lady with her painted face and rouged lips and penciled eyebrows, seated lazily on her haunches and smoking a long red bamboo pipe, emitting faint blue rings of tobacco smoke from her mouth, pretending not to see the crowds of people swarming in front of the cage and yet, catlike, furtively watching their every movement together with the movements of her rival, The Lily, on the further end of the cage. And, while the other women were engaged in whispered conversation about the personal appearance of onlookers but mainly about the beauty and shapeliness of the new *yuyo*. The Lily, the *o shoku* feigned absorption in the perusal of a long epistle supposed to have been sent her by one of her numerous admirers, a poet.

The Lily kept her eye on this *o shoku* continually. She was determined that she was going to learn all that this proud beauty had to offer. So she did not take part in the various other activities in which the other girls were engaged. She did not blow the berry of the winter-cherry between her lips as she had learned to do as a *geisha*. She did not make paper frogs as a charm to attract a man. She did not practice *tatamizan*, that is, divination with mat-straws. She kept her eyes glued on the *o shoku*.

Outside, in the street, the young blades of the city had just started to enter the *Omon* that opened into the confines of the *Yoshiwara*. *Jin-rikshas* pulled up to various establishments, the men puffing from their exertions in pulling their loaded vehicles up the hill that led into the *Omon*. The street began to grow alive with people. It was as though the street took on human attributes and breathed. Vendors of rice dumplings strode up and down crying out their monotonous *"Dango, dango!"* competing with the sellers of boiled red beans, *ude-adzuki*, fruit, *midzu gashi*, sake, *sushi*, which were rice-cakes plastered over with fish or seaweed in which vinegar had been sprinkled and numerous other delicacies. *Tsuji-ura* sellers sold their small pieces of paper on which printed poems were wrapped in cracknels of rice. News-paper sellers, fortune-tellers, *uranai-sha*, boiled bean sellers, *tofu* sellers, blind shampooers, fe-male hairdressers, washermen, messengers, *shinnai kappore* dancers, singers of the *hayari-uto*, popular songs, *shodara-kyo*, reciters of com-ic imitations of the Buddhistic writings and prayers, and the *shaku-hachi* flute players

134

all contributed their cries and their shrieks and their jargon to make up what was the song of the *Yoshiwara*. Beggars swarmed in front of the smaller brothels, attempting to ransack the remnants of food left over by the guests, clawing hungrily and devouring the leftovers like pigs.

Such was the character of the street in front of the brothel in which The Lily was now displayed. And as time went by the number of people increased until there was a veritable jam streaming past the cages. Still no guest had entered the brothel. All of the *yuyo* were on edge. The *o shoku* was smiling confidently, assured of the fact that, because she was *o shoku*, she would be the first *yuyo* to be called for duty. Everyone knew that the *o shoku*, because she was the first and chief prostitute, the *oiran* in other words, would be the first to be called.

Suddenly, the *bantu* came shuffling in from the back entrance of the cage that led into the *hiki-tsuke-zashiki*, or introduction chamber. Everyone knew that he had come to call the name of the *yuyo* whose services were required by an awaiting guest. But none of the *yuyo* deigned even to listen. They all knew that the name of the *o shoku* would be called. Twenty heads went up. Twenty heads turned in the direction of *Ito Shin*, the *bantu*. Twenty mouths fell open with astonishment when they heard the clerk announce: "The presence of the honorable Lily is desired in the *hiki-tsuke-zashiki*."

The *o shoku's* eyes widened with surprise. Then they quivered as though she were attempting to stifle a tear. There was a plot against her, she felt. They were trying to take her status of *oiran* away from her and give it to this newcomer of an upstart, The Lily. But whatever it was that was moiling in her mind, her still, formalized features gave no sign of the rancor that had been stirred within her. Instead, she smiled bitterly and contemplated the crowd of people that still surged past the cage.

The Lily, however, rose demurely from her place and, with the strange smile at the corners of her mouth and the proud glimmer in her eyes, she stepped to the entrance and disappeared from the cage. While she was still there, a silence brooded over the cage. But, immediately, when she had left, the other *yuyo* set up a chatter like a cage of monkeys so that the *yarite* had to come rushing into the cage and threaten them with beatings and fines unless they quieted down. This done, she stepped up to the *oiran* and there conversed with her in low tones so that the gist of their talk might not be overheard by the rest of the girls.

Meanwhile, The Lily, led by the *bantu*, was taken into the introducing chamber. On entering, she saw an elaborately decorated room. An alcove to one side housed a *kakemono* representing a rising sun and stork. The ceiling was painted with an enormous phoenix. Candles were lighted. But most important of all, The Lily saw, seated on the floor, a very old man. Beside him, there sat another guest, but he, contrarily, was very young. And, as if to take up wasted time, he was rapidly sketching on a pad of paper the figure of the older man, dozing his head nodding. By the side of the older man stood an empty sake bottle.

Upon her entrance, the young man suddenly looked up from his sketching as though to take another glimpse of his model. But when he saw The Lily standing in the doorway, he drew no more. His eyes were on her constantly. The *bantu* pointed at The Lily as if to say, "This is she of whom we spoke." The younger man leaned over and gently nudged the sleeper. "Master, master!" he said softly.

The old man tried to shake off the younger one's proddings by grunting and attempting to fall asleep again. But the younger one insistently nudged him, calling out, "Master, master!"

Finally, the old man managed to get his eyes opened. That is, he opened only one eye and peered from under heavy eyebrows at his young companion. "How dare you awaken me from my sake sleep?"

The younger man nodded to The Lily with his head. "She is here, master, she is here!"

"Who is here who is more important than my sake sleep?" the older man grumbled sleepily and closed his one eye again.

"The beautiful *oiran* of whom the *kutsuwa* of this brothel spoke, master!"

Again the old man opened his eye slowly and turned it in the direction of The Lily. Immediately, his other eye opened widely. He drew his chin up and away from his chest. All that he said was, "Ah-h!" Then, for a whole minute, he stared at The Lily, saying not a word but going over her every line and point of beauty.

When he had apparently completed his external survey, in the cracked voice of an old man, he asked, "What is your name, O honorable flower that blossoms in the mire?"

The Lily half-closed her eyes when she answered, "The Lily."

"I am *Utamuro!*" and when he said it, the the old man scrutinized the girl's face to see whether or not it had made any affect on her. Apparently, it had not, for he made a sour face and he sucked his tongue into his mouth and massaged his toothless gums with it.

But the name had meant something to The Lily. She had heard of the great artist, *Utamuro*, during her days at the *geisha* school and she had admired his work considerably, not only because of the artistic quality, but because the subjects and the subject matter, in most cases, had pertained to the *Yoshiwara* and its inhabitants. And so, she replied, "The master *Utamuro's* art has ever been a source of pleasure to this insignificant lover of things artistic!"

A smile now replaced the frown on the great artist's face. "Then you do know of me, eh?" and he nodded his head up and down for no reason at all, like old men usually do. Then, looking her over again minutely, he mumbled to himself, "Not bad, not bad, not bad!"

At that moment, the owner of the brothel came bustling in, rubbing the palms of his hands like a merchant. "And how does the honorable master *Utamuro* find my newest *yuyo?*"

"Excellent!" the master said slowly, still gaping at The Lily.

"Shall we adjourn to the young lady's *zashiki?*" the owner suggested, for he not only desired to consummate the present negotiations but guests were already entering and he was now in sore need of the introducing room in which they were seated.

Utamuro extended his hands to the young man. "Help me up, *Kaisho!* We shall accompany the young lady to her *zashiki* to accomplish our purpose."

The younger man leaped up from his squatting position and took hold of the old man's hand and slowly drew him up to his feet, as the old man groaned and squirmed, complaining how roughly he was being handled. This accomplished, he waved The Lily away, "Lead us to thy room, oh fairest flower who men call The Lily!" As The Lily turned and left the room, the old man followed her, leaning heavily on the arm of the younger man who saw nothing but the undulant swaying of The Lily's buttocks as she ascended the stairs a few steps ahead of them and heard nothing but the clippity-clop of her sandals clattering on the wood.

In the room, the old artist demanded that he be deposited in a position directly opposite The Lily's *kuton* bed of mattresses. This done, the young man whose name was *Kaisho* remained standing, awaiting further orders from his master. The Lily likewise stood still next to her *kuton* and with her hands on her hips, the peculiar smile in her eyes and mouth, she also awaited the first command. In reality, she was extremely disappointed. She felt that her first paid brothel fuck should at least have been a young man capable of making her earn the three *yen* the brothel was going to receive instead of an old man who had to be helped to his feet. Now, that young man who was with the old man. What was his name? *Kaisho*. He would be different. This would be a messy job. The young man would have to extend the old man's penis and, like the mating of a wild stallion with a mare, insert the flaccid tool into The Lily's hole. There would be no pleasure, no passion, no love. Only work, hideous work.

But her pique at being so deceived almost vanished when she saw the younger man hand the older one the sketch pad and the brush with which he had been previously sketching down in the introducing room. For a moment, the old man regarded the sketches that the younger had made. Suddenly he burst out, "This line, this line, pig! Have you forgotten all that I have taught you?"

"But master," the young man protested, "the light was not what it should have been!"

"To an artist, light means nothing. His technique, his knowledge of line, his feeling for form should be in his fingertips and not in his eyes!" And the old man set to finding more errors in the sketch, never praising and completely forgetting the presence of The Lily. Suddenly ,he caught himself. "Oh, a thousand pardons!" he exclaimed. "Come, *Kaisho*, we must to our work!" He turned the page of sketches to the rear of the pad and prepared a clean sheet. "I have come here, fairest Lily, because thy master has informed me of thy beauty of form and face." Here he blew his nose into his fingers before continuing. "He has not exaggerated, eh *Kaisho?*"

The young man merely nodded his head in assent.

Then they were, the three of them, the young man standing by the side of the artist, the young girl standing by the side of her bed, the old man seated on the floor, a pad of sketch paper on his lap, his brush poised in the air like a heron about to make a swift dive downward to spear a fish in the flashing rapids of a mountain stream.

"Well!" the old man barked.

"What must I do?" The Lily asked.

Again the old man became apologetic. "Again I must beg of you a thousand pardons. Let me explain to you, oh honorable flower. Last year, there came to my humble domicile a count, the Count of *Mito.* And he demanded of me that I paint for him a scroll of the *Yoshiwara* in which are depicted a beautiful *yuyo* like yourself and a man in poses of passion and love. It seems that this Count must first gaze at such pictures before he is able to have an erection and thus be enabled to make use of the hundred and one concubines he owns. For a year he has been annoying me for the silken scroll. For a year I have been putting him off. Art cannot be bought for so many *yen.* Art cannot be commissioned for such and such a time. Art can be created only when the mood is in one, when the artist has been inspired. At last I have been inspired. Heretofore, I have had access to only the usual *oiran*. But when your master told me of you, I hastened immediately here to see you. I repeat, at last I am inspired. I have brought *Kaisho* along with me. He is one of my best pupils. He is young. He shall be your paramour. You shall be his *yuyo*. I shall limn you both and, in the deathless strokes of my art, I shall preserve these next hours for posterity!" He panted now from the exertion of his many words and laved his parched lips with his tongue and sucked them into his toothless gums. "The sake shall wait. The urge is in my blood. I feel a masterpiece coming on me!" And with these words, he brought the pendant brush down to the white expanse of virgin paper. A smoothly flowing black line showed when he lifted the brush up again. "Come!" he cried impatiently, "you are not sticks! You are man and woman!"

Kaisho walked slowly over to the *kuton* where The Lily was standing. Hesitantly, he extended his hand as if to untie her *obi*. He drew it back again fearfully when he heard the old man shrill out, "Stop! she must be dressed. Suggestion. Suggestion, lout! How many times have I taught you that the crux of Japanese art is suggestion. We must not inform the Prince blatantly that The Lily has a beautiful body. We must suggest it to him. Then his brain will conceive it as being even more beautiful than it really is. Suggestion! Suggestion!" and he again dropped his head to the sheet of paper mumbling, "suggestion, suggestion!"

Like a pair of strange dogs sniffing themselves for identification, *Kaisho* and The Lily first handled each other. Very delicately, *Kaisho* took The Lily's hand and drew her down to the mattresses. Very demurely, as though it were a rite from the tea ceremony, The Lily allowed herself to be seated on the *kuton*. She was going to have a real fuck, she knew. *Kaisho* was young. *Kaisho* was much taller than the average Japanese. *Kaisho* was seriously affected by the close contact with The Lily for, jutting under his robe, she saw a hump that amply foretold of what she was to expect from him in the way of a man-sized prick.

Kaisho was also an artist. He knew exactly what it was that his master desired. So, instead of entering into The Lily directly between her legs, he lifted her right leg high up into the air. Then, with his free hand, he withdrew his prick from his robe and held it enticingly in front of The Lily's throbbing cunt. For the moment she was in a quandary. Why did he hold his luscious tool in front of her without skirmishing around her clitoris first so as to titillate her into passion? Why did he pose with it in his hand? And then the answer came to her troubled questions, came to her when she looked over to the old man and saw him sketching them industriously. Suddenly, she felt the tip of his prick insinuate itself into the lips of her vagina. But, strangely enough, it went no further. Instead of sinking his prick to the hilt, as was to be expected of him, he seemed to be content to allow it merely to rest, its point barely sunk into the luxuriant growth of pubic hairs, its throbbing tip seemingly immune to the violent actions of her cunny, drawing, sucking, pulsating madly in an attempt to draw his prick deeper into her. The Lily was unable to stand this inaction. In her there was a man's prick. In her there was a crazy desire for the act. In her there boiled a seething caldron of action. And so she began to gyrate her ass and thrust her cunt forward with spasmodic jerks, attempting vainly to work his prick deeper into her avid hole. "Deeper, deeper!" she finally managed to cry out, her inhibited passions getting the most of her, the threat of tears in her voice.

But *Kaisho* seemed not to hear her plea. Instead, he stared stonily at his master, waiting for the sign from him which would send him into the next position.

The Lily became frantic. Passion was tearing her insides apart. Passion was making her legs quiver like a reed in the wind. Passion was sending her deep sobs into her throat, tears into her eyes, turmoil into her mind. Was this a stick in her? Was he not a man? Could he not sense that she wanted him to fuck her masterfully now, as a man should fuck, as a woman should be fucked? She threw her arms around his neck and kissed him again and again on the lips and on the eyes and on his throat, trying to show him that she was his slave and master, pitifully demeaning herself to him so that he would give her that for which she was aching.

But still *Kaisho* heeded her not. He went no further than he had been at first. "Brute, beast!" she wept to him, the great tears welling over her eyes and coursing down her cheeks. And she beat her tiny fists against his chest pitifully. For the moment, it appeared as though *Kaisho* could hold out no longer. For, already he felt the suggestion of an urge at the root of his prick and, in his balls, there appeared that slight commotion that presaged an orgasm. Besides, the pretty young thing below him was maddeningly provocative now that she was weeping and entreating him to insert his prick further and beating his chest so prettily. To himself, he hoped fervently that the master would either complete the sketches or else . . . else . . . and he looked up at the master when he heard what he thought was a snore. Yes. The master's head had fallen to his chest. Deep, stentorian rumbles were issuing from his open mouth. His brush hand had fallen to his side and the brush, still held tightly between his thumb and forefinger, had smeared a long line across the page of sketches as it had swooped downward the moment the artist's conscious mind had given in to the inexorable demands of the sleeping unconscious mind.

Kaisho gave his body a slight shove forward and then stared intently at the master. But *Utamuro* seemed to give no sign of awakening. Again *Kaisho* thrust himself forward a trifle. And again he searched his master's face intently for a sign. Then, being satisfied that they would not be disturbed, *Kaisho* turned to The Lily.

"Now, beautiful Lily, now I shall demonstrate to you that I am no stone!" And, with these words, he took The Lily's body up in his arms and drew her as close as he possibly could and almost squeezed the breath out of her. "Now do you feel my manhood growing in you?" Suiting the action to the words, he began a series of violent thrusts, inserting his prick deeper and deeper into The Lily's cunny, until panting with exertion, he dropped his head to The Lily's breast and nuzzled her nipples like a child.

Smiles twinkled behind the tears in The Lily's eyes now. The little man in her had come to life. Swollen now to the right size, she felt *Kaisho's* prick rub the sides of her cunny and, occasionally, butt up against the uppermost part of it. The wait was worth all of the tears and anguish. For the pleasure was magnified all the more now that she was finally being fucked. Back and forth she worked her ass. Frantically she manipulated the wonderful muscles in her quim. Wildly she gyrated her cunt, twirling his prick in her like a cat twirls a hapless mouse. Madly she rolled her eyes and panted and quivered in the throes of an intense inundation of passion.

Then he came.

Then she came.

On the floor, the master artist chuckled silently to himself, closed the one eye that he had opened when he had feigned slumber to watch the antics of this young pair of fools, and prepared himself for a real nap for the night.

The Lily and *Kaisho* had thrown their arms around each other and were bathing themselves in the afterthroes that come in the wake of a severe period of fucking.

In the arms of the artist apprentice, *Kaisho,* The Lily heard the noises from the street outside diminish. The crowd of *Yoshiwara* loafers, the *hiyakashi,* dispersed one by one and nothing but the faint cries of an occasional macaroni seller crying his wares and a blind shampooer's call of *"amma-hari"* came into the stillness of the night. Once in a while the dismal howling of a moonstruck mongrel pierced the brittle night and shattered it into a thousand pieces.

But on the bed of mattresses, The Lily and *Kaisho* loved.

On the floor, the master artist, *Utamuro* slept and snored.

CHAPTER 9

When we left The Lily in the last chapter, she was already assured of the position of *oiran* of a minor first-class brothel. Taking her life up now in this chapter, we find that she has attained the coveted position of chief *oiran* in the highest-class brothel in the *Shin-Yoshiwara*. And we have traversed only the period of one year. Think of that, my friends. To be able to attain such honor in the short course of one year. But she was The Lily. And that, in itself, should explain her phenomenal rise.

During that year, she had managed to make herself known as the most expert prostitute in the kingdom. Men traveled miles, hundreds of miles, merely to see her. Travel-worn and weary, the dust of the *Tokaido* on their torn clothing, they paid their last *kotsu* just to see her. They felt, like the Mohammedans feel about Mecca. One had to see Mecca and then die. One had to see The Lily and then one could die happily.

During this year there came many men to partake of the luscious feast of love that The Lily provided. But none, none was so satisfying to The Lily as was the great *Shirai Gompachi.* For *Gompachi* was a wrestler. Now wrestlers all over the world are supposed to be huge, monstrous hulks of men. In Japan they are no less. In Japan, however, our wrestlers are not as tall as are the Occidental ones. But what they lack in height they make up in girth for it seems that the larger the belly in a Japanese wrestler, or *sumotori,* the better wrestler he is. In Japan, weight counts most, although most people believe that with *jiu-jitsu* weight is unnecessary. But there are two kinds of wrestlers in Japan. And the champion wrestlers are those who wrestle twice a year in Tokyo for the national championships.

The point is that *Gompachi* was an enormous man with an enormous appetite, both gastronomically and sexually, with an enormous belly to take care of his sexual appetite. He, too, had heard of The Lily. And when he came directly to the brothel instead of to the *hikite-jaya* as most important men did, the *yarite* and the *bantu* and the owner all crowded around him as he waited in the introducing room and rubbed their hands together in anticipation of the money that this famous wrestler was going to leave them before the morning came around.

The Lily came walking down the stairs majestically. She was attired now in a long loose *shikake*, a robe made of black material that is worn only by the *o shoku kabu*, the chief courtesan in the best house of the *Yoshiwara*. To The Lily, *Gompachi* was a *shokwai no kyaku*, that is to say, a strange guest whom she had not been introduced to before with the regular form of *hikisuke*. The Lily eyed the wrestler gravely through half-closed eyelids. The wrestler stared at The Lily with wide-open eyes, the passion in them only too evident. His great hand opened and closed convulsively. Almost involuntarily, he laved his lips with his tongue as though he were already experiencing the pleasure of The Lily's charms in his mind.

The introduction over, the servants cried out, "*O meshi-kae, o meshi-kae*," which indicated that now was the time for the honorable change of garments by The Lily. Immediately, she ascended to her room, changed her clothing from the black robe to a kimono that was made of *moyo mono*, a figured material. Then she descended again to *Gompachi*, whose eyes were for no one but her. There, she aided the others in preparing the feast that the wrestler had ordered from the *dai-ya* of the *Kaneko* restaurant.

"I want no ordinary food from a stinking *dai-ya!*" the wrestler had cried impatiently. "Bring me *Kaneko* foodstuffs and nothing else. And so they brought him *no ich-mai ippon* which was an ordinary dish of food with a bottle of sake thrown in, but they came back from the famous *Kaneko* restaurant loaded down with the best of the varied cuisine that it offered. *Takemura no sembei, tsuke-na ni-mame, maku-n-uchi, kanro-bai, hakuro* and *dengakutofu*. Were I to describe these delicacies to you in English, I know that I would make your honorable mouths water. And so I shall merely let this description stand, assuring you that the wrestler did justice to the pile of food-stuffs that was heaped in front of him while The Lily, the half-smile on her face, watched the proceedings, helped at times with the serving and bided the time until she was to serve to *Gompachi* a feast that would surpass this meal by far, a feast of love, a banquet of all the sexual senses.

Finally, when the food was cleared away, when the last bottle of sake and *shopu* and *mirin* were drunk down, the wrestler gave one last bottom-bellied belch, his hands across his stomach and he looked longingly in the direction of The Lily. For the moment there was silence. Then the wrestler said, *"O hike,"* which meant, "Tis the honorable bedtime." Then Lily rose demurely and made her way up the stairs to her room. A couple of *waikemono* jumped forward to help the wrestler to his feet but, with a roar, he pushed them indignantly away, and with a series of grunts he finally managed to get himself up off the floor. With a scowl in the direction of the servants, he started off for the stairway, stumbling on every step. He finally reached the top. "Where art thou, wench?" he called out. And, from the direction of The Lily's room, he heard a tinkling laugh and a, "Here, where thy slave awaits thee!"

When he stopped into the doorway of The

Lily's *zashiki*, he saw her awaiting him near her *kuton*, attired in a nightdress of a striped material that seemed to cling to her lithe body and outlined individually every one of her charms. With arms outstretched, he stumbled over to her and dragged her down to the bed of mattresses with him. He could not bide his time now. He could not waste the precious seconds in undressing himself. He knew only that there was a wild urge in him for this provocative woman that was now lying at his side. He knew only, as his fumbling fingers stroked her breasts and touched her already stiffened nipples and finally roamed to the hair of her cunt, that he wanted to fuck this woman as he never before had wanted to fuck his thousands of other women. But The Lily managed to control his desire until she could strip him entirely.

There the pair of them lay, stripped naked, the beautiful, marvelously formed body of The Lily, against the bescarred, tumultously fat body of the wrestler. Hair in great quantities was scattered over his back and his chest and in his crotch. And from between the great bush of his crotch there jutted out as enormous a prick as has ever been graced by a man. There was no describing it. Is there no wonder that The Lily gasped when she saw it pop out of his robe when she undressed him. Now it was only at halfmast. How much longer could it grow, she thought? And, as if to test it, she inserted her fingers underneath the balls and gently tickled that sensitive region.

The big wrestler moaned. Then he threw his

immense arms around The Lily. "I shall fuck you as you have never been fucked before!" he whispered gruffly to her.

"Actions speak louder than words!" The Lily replied.

With a roar, the wrestler made a sudden twist, a wrestler's trick which forced The Lily prone on her back. Then the wrestler began to maneuver his great johnny around. But his belly was so large that he could not see where to place his prick. The Lily smiled up at him as though he were a child. "Must I direct thy stream like a mother directs her babe?" she taunted him. But she took hold of his prick and gently skirmished her hole before inserting it. Then she allowed the tip to enter and she took her hand away. "Now is thy chance!" she whispered to him.

But either the mighty wrestler was too drunk to have control of his penis or else his ponderous belly jutted too far out in front of him for, try as he would, he was unable to insert his prick any further than where The Lily had placed it. He squealed, he grunted, he farted, he sweated. But there she lay, her arms trying to hold on to his enormous girth, her cunny throbbing in preparation for the entrance of that great charger. But there was no entrance. Finally, *Gompachi* lay back on his haunches exhausted. There came a silly grin into his face and he held his hands up as though to say, "I'm sorry, but that's as far as I can go."

But The Lily was not to be so forestalled. Her passion had been aroused by the sight of that great tool. She was going to have it rambling in her or she would know the reason why. So, squirming out from under the great hulk of a man, she turned him around so that he lay on his back. Then, she spread her legs wide apart, and, manlike, she slid her own tiny body into the aperture of his outspread thighs. His stiff prick stuck up out of his belly like a palm tree from a clump of tall grass. Then, carefully adjusting her position, she inserted the cock into her cunt and began to seat herself slowly, impaling herself on the outstretched penis like a chicken on a basting iron.

Thus, she worked herself up and down, and each time she came down she allowed his prick to sink a little deeper into her until, by the time she grew tired from her unaccustomed exertions, she felt that she was touching bottom. Meanwhile, the wrestler *Gompachi* had recovered some of his senses when he saw that paragon of a woman bouncing up and down on his prick like a little monkey on a stick. He reached out his great hands and fondled her breasts until they stood up like soldiers, full and proud. Then, as if to help her when he saw that she was tiring, he took hold of her waist and helped her in her motions, lifting her up when she found it necessary to do so, and allowing her to drop on the rebound, as though he were tossing a baby on his knee.

This went on for some time because, with the alcohol in his system, the wrestler found it difficult to spend his load, although The Lily was thankful that he didn't. For she was experiencing that sensation that comes with satiety. She felt that never before had she been fucked. All the other times were only exercises, preparations for this one grand fuck of the century. And so she squirmed and twisted on his prick, plying all of the arts that she had learned at the *geisha* school and from the *hokan,* until she worked herself up to a pitch where she was unable to control her own passions. And the emotions in her piled up one on top of the other until they reached their peak and spilled over within her in one grand, overwhelming second of unalloyed bliss. But still the prick within her was hard and solid and long and jounced her innards like mad. So that, although she had reached one climax already, she found herself well on the way to another one. This had never happened to her before. And so, again working her ass and cunt with that cunning technique, she continued the action again and again. Finally, she came again. And this time, wonder of all wonders, she felt a great spending within her, a great warmth of liquid spurting up and splashing against every corner of her womb. And she knew that the wrestler had come with her.

And she sank down exhaustedly to his belly.

With her head in her arms, she allowed herself to fall into a light sleep, her arms resting on the mountainous pile of flesh that stuck up immediately in front of her.

That was her *shokwai,* her first meeting with *Gompachi.* After that, he spent much of his time in the *Yoshiwara.* He became her favorite lover for, when he was not drunk, he knew how to handle his oversized cock as no other man did.

It was at this time, however, that The Lily had an odd experience. For some time she had been feeling only the extensive size of great cocks like the wrestler's in her. Suddenly, like a pregnant woman who desires the oddest things at the oddest times of the night, a strange desire came over her for the feel of a small penis, a boy's penis. And this desire was fulfilled by a young son of the brothel owner who, contrary to all rules, had wandered upstairs in search of adventure.

He found it in The Lily's room.

It being early in the afternoon, she was still asleep. Suddenly, she felt in her sleep that there was a presence in the room with her. She opened her eyes slowly to see the figure of a young boy of about ten standing in front of her. His eyes were glued to the jewel between her legs, for, during the night, she had thrown the covering back and her nightdress had been flung open, thus revealing her delightful cunny sparkling behind its veil of hair.

She smiled up at the lad.

He smiled back at her.

"Do you like it?" she asked, spreading her legs a trifle apart so that more of the splendors of that marvelous cunt could be discerned by the now gasping youngster.

The young boy could not even nod his head, so engrossed was he with the marvels that were being revealed to him. He felt his mouth go dry and he swallowed hard. And, within him, he felt a funny feeling. And the thing that he pissed from, strangely, was growing larger and stiffer.

The Lily extended her hand to him, took hold of his arm and drew him closer to her. Then, inserting a hand in the open fold of his robe, she searched around until she brought to view the head of his ridiculously small boy's penis. But it was stiff and rigid.

"Do you know what this is for, little boy?" she asked.

Again he could not say a word. Nor did he say a word when The Lily took the little thing into her mouth and tongued it for all she was worth. Still the little boy did not come. She marveled at it and tickled him under his balls. Then, taking him by the waist as *Gompachi* had done to her, she lifted him up and settled him directly into her cunt. Physically, there was no sensation. She felt only as though there was a worm wriggling in her. She was about to be disappointed when a novel idea came to her. Clapping her hands together, she summoned the young *shinzo* who aided her in her toilet and ran her errands for her. The *shinzo* entered shyly. She was about ten years old, too. And when she saw the young lad on her mistress' belly, she blushed and tried to back away. But The Lily called out imperiously to her. "Come here, *Akika*. I have work for you."

With these words, she took the boy off of her belly and took hold of the young girl's hand and drew her, too, down on the mattress. Then, spreading the little girl's legs wide apart, she indicated to the boy that he should insert his little penis into her little hole. The boy hesitated, not knowing what to do. And so, The Lily, taking hold of the little thing, drew it down and put it into the *shinzo's* aperture. Nature then came to the fore in the lad. And with the movements that would have done justice to an old cocksman, he wiggled his little ass around. The little girl, having seen her mistress ply her trade many times, emulated her and received his thrusts with a professional touch. Watching their antics, The Lily felt an urge within her growing. And having no male with which she could practice copulation, she inserted her finger into her cunt and titillated her clitoris until it rose like a stiff prick. Even this was not enough for her so she edged over to the little girl's head and squatted down over her so that her cunt sank down into the *shinzo's* mouth. And, the little girl, knowing what was demanded of her, inserted her tongue into her mistress' cunny and tongued her clitoris until, finally, she heard The Lily moan with passion and, a second later, let loose a flood of pearly essences. At the same time, the little fellow came into the girl and the girl felt an orgasm explode within her. Then together, the three of them threw their arms around each other and rested from their exhausting efforts.

It came to pass, during The Lily's stay at the *Yoshiwara* that there came a gentleman. And this gentleman, although he was not of the nobleman's class, appeared to be of them. For he held himself erect, and deigned not to look at the menials of the establishment but directed imperiously that he speak to the *kutsuwa* of the brothel and the *kutsuwa* only. Immediately upon being informed by the *bantu* that a gentleman desired to speak to him, the *kutsuwa* came shuffling out of the *yarite's* room where they had been talking over the success of The Lily.

It evolved that the gentleman was the personal secretary to the Count of *Mito*. His lord and master desired that The Lily be prepared to be taken to the *hikite-jaya* where the Count was awaiting her. Immediately there was a hustle and a bustle. A Count was asking the favors of the house. The Lily had drawn the attention of the nobility. And when they finally were completed with her, there was no more beauteous *oiran* in the history of the *Yoshiwara*. Her upper garment consisted of white *nanako* dyed with purple clouds among which peeped out some swirling patterns. And all about were flowers embroidered in silk and finished by hand paintings of the four seasons in vivid colors with a crest of a *wistaria* flower sewn onto the dress with purple thread. Her underwear consisted of figured satin bordered with plain brown *hachijo* silk and embroidered with the same pattern in colored silk. And her lower girdle was of claret-colored figured satin lined with bright scarlet silk crepe. Her nightgown, which was carried carefully by her *shinzo* behind her, was a garment of scarlet crepe trimmed with purple figured satin and edged with gold and silver threads so as to give the effect of waves breaking upon the seashore while her nightsash was of *kabe-choro*, wrinkled silk. Around her was flung a *shikake*, a cloak with a pattern in it representing a cloud with lightning and a golden dragon, embroidered in gold.

Is there no wonder that the Count gasped and took a step backward when he saw this beautiful apparition being led by his secretary into the private room that he had apportioned out in the *hikite-jaya?* The Count was rather tall for a Japanese. But there was something about his bearing, something about the majestic haughtiness of the man that indicated that he was of the nobility. For the while he did nothing but go over The Lily's charms as she stood in the door awaiting word from him. Then he said slowly, chopping his words out, like a man who has been accustomed to having his orders obeyed.

"So you are The Lily."

The Lily only lowered her eyes in respect.

The Count continued, "Some time ago I commissioned an artist to paint a beautiful woman for me. The world acclaims *Utamuro* as a great artist. He is not. The scrolls he drew up for me are poor compared to the original." And then, in a husky voice that dripped with passion, he snarled out, "Clear the room, dogs! I would be alone with this flower!"

In a moment they were alone.

The Count drew The Lily down upon the *kuton* that had been prepared for them. "My concubines are pigs compared to you. For with them I must needs stimulate my desire first with pictures. But with you, I need no pictures. I need only you!" And as he spoke these words, the note of command seemed to have dropped away from them. With The Lily at his side, he became an ordinary man. His hand avidly searched beneath her clothing for her breasts.

He fondled them, feeling the nipples rise under his manipulations. With his free hand, he went under the outer clothing and the underclothing until his fingers became entangled with the hair of her cunny. Then, firmly, he inserted his finger into the aperture and felt around for her clitoris. As this was going on, The Lily had taken his face into her hands and had dropped her mouth to his, where she entwined her tongue in his tongue and kissed him violently again and again. By this time, the Count had found her button and was busily engaged in diddling it, occasionally inserting his finger deeper into her vagina, working himself up to a pitch of passion so that, before long, he was breathing as heavily as a lad newly fucked.

"You stir me, wonderful flower!" he whispered to her.

"Stir me!" she whispered back to him.

In response, he took her hand, directed it into his robe and placed the fingers around his prick. It was not exactly limp, for signs of life were beginning to throb through it, but it was hardly stiff enough to warrant its being able to be thrust into The Lily's cunt.

She smiled to him. "Is that all?" she asked. Then, taking the prick out from its hiding place, she brought her mouth down over it and began to suck it. First, with tiny love-kisses, she covered its entire length, dropping even below the bottom of the prick to the balls, nibbling gently, tickling them with her free hand. Life, practically nil until that time, became evident now. With this kissing of the prick accomplished, The Lily popped the penis into her mouth. First she went no further than the head, allowing her tongue to encircle it like a ring of flame. Then, at timed intervals, she would allow her mouth to fall lower and lower over the stiffening prick, compressing her lips a trifle with each upward stroke so that the walls of her mouth rubbed against the sides of his prick. And, as she drew upwards, she would create a suction in her mouth by sucking inwards.

The Count was delighted at this turn of affairs. Heretofore it had taken hours for his concubines to work his prick up to a hard-on. But now, within the short space of fifteen minutes, his prick was as hard as wood and, within him, there was boiling that desire for contact with a woman. Again he inserted his fingers into her cunt and searched diligently for her clitoris, finding it finally and drawing it out so that it stiffened under his fingers. By this time, his prick had already reached the point where it could be inserted quite readily. And so, adjusting her position once more, The Lily drew her underclothing aside and laid bare the jewelbox in which she guarded her sexual treasures. "Here is the proper receptacle for the new thing you have discovered to be dangling between your legs, master!"

The Count stared down into the lovely cunny.

"Your cunny hair is not as dark as your other hair," he said, and then he continued. "I have home a young lady whose cunny hair is golden and she is a marvelous fuck!"

The Lily smiled. Then she said, punning, "All is not gold that clitoris, master!"

The Count could control himself no longer. Taking his distended staff in hand, he spread wide The Lily's legs, spread open the outer lips of her cunny with the thumb and forefingers of his left hand and, with his right hand, took hold of his tool and directed it into the hole that gaped for it. For him this was practically a new sensation. Heretofore, he had been forced to fuck with a quasihard prick because he had seldom been able to raise a real erection. And, as one concubine stretched his prick out, they would both attempt to shove it into the orifice of another concubine. How unsatisfactory it all had been, he mused, as he felt his taut cock slide sinuously into the hot receptacle of the beautiful woman below him, like a piston. Now there was pleasure. Now there was happiness. And he pushed and withdrew his prick in and out while he cupped The Lily's breasts in his hands and molded them in his fingers. And he was not alone in motion for, as was her usual wont, The Lily began to practice those sexual gymnastics that she had learned from the *hokon* in the *geisha* school. From side to side with a lascivious motion, she twirled her hips so that the friction of the walls of her vagina against the sides of his prick was augmented. Then, in addition to these sidewise motions, she injected variety, receiving the violent thrusts of his prick with a motion that made it appear to him as though his prick had sunk a thousand miles into a seat of downy cushions. And then, as he felt the tip of his prick reveling in the luscious depths of an effulgent warmth that seemed like warm honey, she would give her cunt muscles a slight twitch which sent a sort of electrical current shooting up the entire length of his prick, into his vitals and up his spine so that he almost shuddered in the pain of joy.

He came in a spurt such as he had never before experienced.

But that was not all.

Lying limp in her wet, warm cunny, he felt his prick revel in the afterthroes of the fuck. And then, with a subtlety that wormed its way almost unnoticeably into his very being, he felt those marvlous sphincter muscles begin their work. He felt the gentle, insistent curling of tense fingers explore his cock like the tentacles of a squid. He felt rising within him a resurgence of latent power that he never before had imagined or experienced in himself. One fuck a night had ever been more than enough. But here, here he felt his prick take on once more the semblance of a cock ready for action. Twice in one night? It was incredible, he thought, unbelievable. A miracle! Yet, sure enough, as he lay outstretched on the body of The Lily, his hands exploring her breasts, her tongue darting into his mouth, her cunt muscles milking him slowly but surely, he knew that he was going to experience that fine sensation once more. And, as he thought of those pleasant things, he felt his prick grow harder and harder. And, before he was completely aware of it, he realized that his prick had regained its former strength and was lying ready to be thrust once more in and out of the receptacle in which it had been rejuvenated.

Was it no wonder that he recommended the Baron *Sochi* to her the moment he got in touch with that great personage and confidante of the *Mikado* himself?

The Baron came the next evening. He was a middle-aged man, short, with a sizeable belly and always out of breath as though he were continually exerting himself. He, too, sent his man to The Lily's brothel to ask for her. Again she was attired in the finest that the *kutsuwa* was able to gather together. Again she was brought into the *hikite-jaya*, followed by her *shinzo* carrying the nightgown which she had not used the night before.

Again, the finest of foods were prepared at the best *dai-ya* in the *Yoshiwara* and delivered where The Lily was entertaining the Baron. And after the repast had been eaten and the sake had been drunk, the servants discreetly disappeared from the room, clearing off the dishes and dinner paraphernalia. And the little *shinzo* laid out the beautiful nightdress with the magnificent *obi* on the *kuton*. And she, too, bowed herself discreetly out of the room, leaving The Lily alone with the Baron.

This time, The Lily was forced to be naked in the Baron's presence. But he insisted on divesting her clothing himself. And, as he disrobed her, he would kiss that part of her body that showed first. So that, when he came to take off the girdle she wore, leaving bare the triangle of love, he bent his head down and sank his mouth deeply into her cleft, his tongue outstretched stiffly so that it entered her cunt almost like a stiff prick. The Lily spread her legs wider in order to facilitate his tonguing of her clitoris, and she reached around and took his stiffening pecker into her hands and fondled it expertly, rubbing it up and down and occasionally giving tiny tweaks to the bottom of his ball sac.

"Why should you give me all the pleasure, honorable master?" she asked of the Baron when he came up once for air.

"I have not finished tonguing your button," he answered.

"Why can I not tongue your staff while you tongue my button?" she asked archly. And as though he had already given assent to her demand, she adjusted their positions on the mattress bed so that, laying belly to belly, his head fell right into the aperture of her cunt and her head was face to face with his prick. Immediately, they each set to working on each other, the Baron continuing in his interrupted tonguing of The Lily's clitoris, The Lily taking the Baron's prick into her mouth and, with a bobbing of her head, sucking it off feverishly.

This double-barrelled action of sucking and being sucked at the same time could result in only one thing. Neither could control his or her emotions. And, before they were fully aware of the consequences both had blown off their passions almost at the same time. As they turned around, the Baron looked ruefully at his weakened penis.

"Curse me for being a weakling!" he muttered.

"Why do you curse yourself, honorable lord?"

"Here I have come already and it will be fully a day before I can steel myself to another hard-on," he replied.

The Lily gave a slight laugh at this and said, "We shall see about that," and taking the limp prick into her mouth once more, she began to tongue it expertly, kissing it delicately at times and mauling it with tight-lipped sucking actions at other times. These actions, however, served only to stiffen the Baron's prick slightly.

"I told you so," the Baron said, shaking his head.

But The Lily did not heed what the Baron said. With a quick change, she drew her mouth away from the Baron's prick. Then, dropping her torso down lower so that she could insert the Baron's half-soft penis into her cunny, she did so, but she still held it in her fingers so that it would not slip out. Then, whirling her hips she set out to regain the former condition of the prick. Subtly, she would contract her sphincter muscles at timed intervals. And, with each contraction, the Baron's prick would take an extra spurt. Finally, almost exhausted from this hard work, The Lily dropped all of her body motions and confined herself merely to the action of those marvelous milking muscles in her cunt. Almost instantaneously now, the Baron's prick grew harder. And the Baron marveled at feeling his manhood rise again. He embraced her tightly with his arms and kissed her madly on the lips again and again. His hands wandered down to her breast; he nibbled lovingly at her nipples so that they, too, rose like a pair of rosebuds.

Finally, the Baron's prick was really stiff and hard.

And, knowing this, The Lily laid back tiredly and allowed the Baron to poke it into her. The sensation was delicious, lying back on the mattress, doing nothing but feeling within her the rousing action of a stiff prick. She felt the Baron's fingers caress her breasts and she felt the Baron's tongue wrap itself around her already stiffened nipples. She felt the Baron's arms entwine themselves around her buttocks. She felt him squeeze her mightily so that her breath was almost taken away. Then she knew that at that point the Baron was about to come once more, was about to spurt his hot semen once more against the throbbing insides of her cunt. And she knew that her work had likewise brought her up to a pitch. She felt the quiet but insistent boiling within her. And she suddenly felt a great splashing within her. And she knew that the Baron had let go.

She, herself, let go!

*　　*　　*

After that, The Lily's time was pretty well taken up exclusively with members of the nobility. Counts, barons, lords, *giin-giin*, that is members of parliament, *taishi*, ambassadors, all came to see The Lily and to be fucked by her. Without exception they all invariably demanded that they be allowed to buy off her bonded indebtedness and have her thus become their own personal concubine. They promised her wonderful things, beautiful kimonos, servants galore, everything. But The Lily was satisfied to remain at the *Yoshiwara*.

It was men that she wanted, not man.

In fact, there was one time that she even tired of these noblemen. Again that strange feeling came over her for something different. She wanted to be fucked by something more elemental than a nobleman. She wanted to smell the honest sweat of an ordinary man. She wanted a change.

And so, one night, contrary to the laws of the *Yoshiwara*, she dressed herself as quietly as possible and, refusing the company of her favorite servant, she prepared to depart for the city, for what she knew not, but she knew only that she had to leave the *Yoshiwara* for the night. The *kutsuwa* and the *yarite* tried to forestall her. But she got her way in the end because they knew that she was a priceless possession to them, for her noblemen clients never left the brothel the next morning without leaving *sobana*, tips for the entire establishment, and they never totaled up the bill of charges but paid handsomely without a murmur.

"But there is a guest waiting downstairs!" the *yarite* cried tearfully, "a real *giin-giin*. He asks only for The Lily!"

"I am tired of impotent *giin-giin!*" The Lily cried. "I want a real man!" and with these words, she turned away and descended the backstairs where a *jinriksha* man was awaiting her quietly.

"*Yaya!*" she commanded.

"*Oi kita, hora yo!*" the *jinriksha* man answered, taking up the shafts of his vehicle, brandishing his *kamban* lantern aloft and starting out for the *Omon*, the great gate that opened onto the highroad that led back to the city.

At a rapid trot, the *jinriksha* man traveled through the gate and out onto the *gojikken-machi* road that led back to the city proper. From the top of the *enn-zaki* hill, The Lily looked back and saw the moated *Yoshiwara* suddenly come to life as the various *hikite-jaya* and brothels and shops lit up their lanterns so that a thousand separate twinkles broke into the darkness like fire-eyes. But The Lily smiled enigmatically to herself and turned around again and commanded the *jinriksha* man to "*Yaka!*" And to herself, she thought of the saying, "The footprints lead into the *Yoshiwara* but seldom out of it," and she knew that she could leave it whenever she chose to, but she didn't choose to, because it was the life she desired most to live.

On and on the *jinriksha* man traveled. Through the countryside and over hills. And as his lithe body rippled with the flexing and unflexing of muscles, The Lily looked down at him and wondered whether she should let him have her. And her nostrils shot up when she got her first whiff of the city. Gradually, the road became more and more populated with houses, until, finally, they found themselves traveling through narrow streets exhaling fetid odors of human bodies and cooking.

It was the *nyubai*, the hot season in Tokyo. The air was heavy with humidity so that the sweat stood out on one's forehead in little beads, and the rotted leather spread mold on one's boots and shoes. Outstanding among the various smells of *daikon* and sewage of human bodies, there was ever present that queer, sickly smell of evergreens.

The *jinriksha* man suddenly stopped.

"Where does the honorable *oiran* wish to be taken?"

The Lily looked down at him. His face was agleam with sweat. Great muscles bunched at his arms and his legs. Thin, sunken cheeks indicated that he was no glutton with food. She thought to herself. He has fucked only *jigoku*, the devilwomen of the streets who carry the beds on their back and are ready for a jump if only for a *kotsu*. For once he shall have a *giin-giin's* woman.

"To thy house, man," she said, lowly.

The man screwed up his features as though he was uncertain as to what he had heard.

"To thy house, fool! *Oide nasen kae?*"

"*So ossesu ga . . .*" the man replied angrily. "You say so but . . ."

The Lily cut into his speech. "*Yabo!* Fool! Do as I command you!"

The *jinriksha* man stared at her for a moment. Then, sullenly, he turned and took up the shafts of his vehicle. "*Itte koyo!*" he replied. "I will go!"

And so, increasing his speed this time, he pulled the *jinriksha* through even narrower streets, blinking with the lights of lanterns behind paper screens. Occasionally, through the dark, the tinkling sound of the *samisen* would sparkle bitterly like a star on a cold, clear night. And a snatch of laughter would appear and disappear. And the smells became all the more apparent while the streets grew narrower until it appeared that the houses on both sides kissed each other.

Finally, they pulled up to an ancient, dilapidated house. All was dark inside. The *jinriksha* man turned. "Here is where I live!" he said sullenly.

"Good, help me down!" The Lily replied giving him her hand. He did so. Then she stood waiting for him. "Why don't you ask me into your domicile, honorable *jinriksha* man?"

The puzzled fellow suddenly took hold of her and said angrily, *"O busharezansu na!* Don't make a fool of me!"

"If you cannot see that I want you to have me," The Lily replied equally angrily, "then you are the fool you accuse yourself of being and not the *sui* I thought you to be!"

Without another word, as his eyes lit up with the light of knowledge, the man suddenly swept her into his arms and carried her into his room. And The Lily nuzzled her nose deep into his sweated armpits and breathed in the odor as though it were the perfume of *Samarkand*.

He laid her down on his bed of rags. "I have not thy *kuton* of down mattresses . . ." he started out apologetically. But, before he could say another word, The Lily interrupted him with, "But thou hast that which I long for, *o kan!*" and she reached between the folds of his blue trousers and searched for his prick.

She found it immediately for it filled up the space of his breeches completely.

"*Chotto mi ne!*" she ejaculated prettily. "Oh, just look at him, "*nan zansu ka?* What is it?"

The answer to her question came immediately for, as she fondled it, it began to take on size until, in a few moments, it had grown to the immense proportions of a cock rampant for action.

After that, they spoke little to each other. For their time was taken up with the serious job of giving each other as much satisfaction as they could in the glorious moments of a fuck. The night was hot and both of them sweated like pigs. But intermingled in the smell of sweat there was also the odor that comes from passion that tickles the nostrils and casts the senses in the throes of an intense emotion of passion. Around her, The Lily noted the poorness of the man's habitat. But in her, she felt the lush richness of his prick poking pleasure into her very innards. This was no weakling nobleman atop of her, she knew. And the muscles that he had grown from his arduous labor served to aid him in making her feel the thrusts of his prick all the more. Here there was no weakling attempt to inject a flaccid member into her avid cunny that longed for a stiff prick, sensate with action and power and virility, all of which she was getting from the alive prick of the *jinriksha* man. Here was a real man, with a real passion for her, with a real prick with which to state that passion both for himself and herself. And she luxuriated in the feeling. She wiggled her ass in accompaniment to his violent thrusts; she used all of her

arts in order to aid him as much as possible.
Finally, after an hour of violent jousting, the
jinriksha man decided that it was time to spurt
his semen. And so, timing himself almost perfectly with her, he splashed his hot juice into
her cunny almost at the same time that she
felt the orgasm tearing her innards apart.

For a while, they lay together thusly, breathing heavily into each other's nostrils, their lips
joined together in an almost inseparable kiss.
The man suddenly felt The Lily grope for his
limp prick. Then he saw her take it into her
hands and start to put it into her mouth. "What
are you doing?" he demanded fearfully of her,
for he thought she was going to bite it off for
him.

She smiled back at him quizzically. "Has
none of your filthy *jigoku* ever taken this into
her mouth?" she asked. He shook his head in
reply.

Then she answered very appropriately, quot-
ing a poem, *"Monosugo ya ara omoshiro no
kaeri-band,* queer, yes, but attractive are the
flowers that bloom out of season . . ." and,
with these words, she popped the thing directly
into her mouth and tongued it like mad until
it again took on the proportions of a man's
prick. So that, when it had reached that status,
she withdrew it and bade him insert it into her
quivering quim. And he did as he was bade,
wondering at the beauties and resourcefulness
of the woman below him.

So they fucked far into the night.

And they fell asleep in each other's arms.

But when he awoke the next morning, the

jinriksha man suddenly remembered upon opening his eyes that he had been sleeping with a beautiful but mad *oiran* from the *Yoshiwara*. And he turned in his rag bed to greet the *houri* with a morning kiss to find only an empty bed. And he scratched his head in wonderment; he puzzled over it all morning. And he decided that it had all been a dream.

But, resting now in her *kuton*, her body cleansed with a hot bath and fragrant with oils and perfumes that her *shinzo* had rubbed her with, The Lily thought back on her escapade. Now she knew that she was satisfied, and she prepared herself for the young nobleman who was awaiting her presence.

CHAPTER 10

Five years have passed.

In the *Yoshiwara,* where time is measured by the number of fornications one has had each night, time passes quickly when one takes an especial delight from fucking, as The Lily did. One wonders how, with all of the fucking she got, that The Lily could have gone at each contact as avidly as she did, as though it were her first sexual thrill. But that was the secret of the success of The Lily. She made every fuck appear to be her first.

Regardless, five years had past. The Lily had become known the world over. In San Francisco, the nostalgic Japanese whom I had occasion to meet during my years spent in America had heard of her and had questioned me as to the verity of the claims made in regard to her charm and beauty and sexual capabilities.

"And can this honorable *oiran* make one fuck three times, even when one is as old as I am?" they would ask of me. And when I would answer them that such was the case, their eyes would become glazed and I could see that they were looking forward to returning to Tokyo as soon as possible.

The Lily had the finest collection of night-clothes throughout the whole of Japan. No other *oiran's* collection of those articles of clothing which distinguished a popular *yuyo* from an ordinary *o-cha wo hiku*, or unpopular one, compared with hers. Of her, the great Japanese poet, *Hiro,* had written: "She is like nothing else on earth . . . words are insufficient to describe her . . . she is beyond words, beyond life, beyond everything . . . she is the eternal symbol of beauty."

Yet it took five years for word of her to get to the ears of the royal family. It happened in this fashion.

The Baron *Sochi,* in honor of the *sori-daijin Kono Heima,* who was prime minister to the *Mikado* himself, had laid plans for a banquet. Included in the varied types of entertainment was The Lily. And although police regulations forbade any *yuyo* from ever leaving the confines of the *Yoshiwara* unless it was to attend the funeral of a relative, nevertheless, because of the position of the principals concerned, The Lily was enabled to entertain the Baron *Sochi's* guests, particularly the Prime Minister, *Kono Heima.*

During the feasting at the banquet, The Lily sat at the side of the Baron *Sochi,* and like the half-dozen other *geisha* girls, washed out the cups for sake for the men and refilled them again from the sake bottle. Afterwards, when the stomachs were filled with food, the minds became filled with lechery. And when their hands began to roam over the bodies of the *geisha* girls, the *geisha* master realized that it was time for the *geisha* performance to begin. And so, calling his flock of girls together, they all went tittering into a side room while the Baron, the Prime Minister and a number of other dignitaries of the State, including a *taishi* who was ambassador to America and a *giin-giin* member of parliament and a *daijin,* a minister of state, lay back on silk *zabutons,* their elbows sunk deep into the cushions, smoking from small-bowled pipes and conversing lewdly on the charms of their individual girls.

Suddenly there came a clap of a hand from the outer room. The men became quiet. A figure entered from the side door. It was *Zenroku,* the *hokan* or male *geisha* who had taught The Lily so much of the art of *gei* and of gymnastic fucking. He entered the room holding a fan in his hand and, after saluting the Prime Minister, closed his fan with a snap and, expressing his obligation to The Lily, said, *"Oiran maido arigato."* Then he bowed low to everyone else in the room. Then, as the men again resorted to sake, he began to jest and buffoon, accompanying his jokes with droll contortions and gesticulations. Faster and faster would his line of witty patter come and all the while he would illustrate his point with sexual movements of his hips and hands until, finally, he had discarded all of his clothing and, in a mad swirling of his body, he danced the *hadaka-odori*, the fuck-dance, going through all of the actions and gesticulations of a man and woman in the throes of a passionate fuck.

All of this was received by the onlookers as very funny. It stimulated them sexually only a trifle for they realized that the real sex stimulant would soon come when The Lily, together with the other *geisha* girls would dance the *chonkina*, that lasciviously lewd dance which was first performed in *Nagasaki*, but which has since been danced all over the world where Japanese congregate in feasting and enjoyment.

The *hokan* finished his dance. A short lull came. Then, three middle-aged women, attired in plain gray kimonos, came out and seated themselves on the floor. Two of them carried *samisens*. The other had a *koto* harp. Immediately, they set to strumming their instruments. First a few sharp notes were struck by the *samisens*, at random it seemed. Then this was followed by a repetition by the *koto*. Then, together, they started on the song proper, accompanied by a burst of ribald, clownish laughter. At that point, six of the *geisha* girls came out of the room posturing stiffly, followed by three little *maiko* girls who were learning the art of *gei*. Theirs was a slow dance with colored handkerchiefs; they moved their bodies and their hands, all the while being accompanied by the almost funereal music made by the five-toned Japanese musical scale.

This *Kappore* dance completed, the little *maiko* vanished into the sideroom and the *geisha* dropped back to the *samisen* women where they continued to gyrate. Into the center of the room walked The Lily now, attired in the finest robe that the *Yoshiwara* had been able to provide. The *samisens* seemed to take on a new note now, a faster note, a note as of the blood pulsing rapidly through the veins. And, to this accompaniment, The Lily danced, using her hands and fingers and hips and, in fact, every portion of her anatomy to tell the story of her dance, which was a sad story, for it was the story of a young girl of the *Yoshiwara* whose lover died in trying to obtain sufficient money to buy her out of her slavery in the *Yoshiwara*.

The dance ended, the *samisens* took up the chords of a new song. It was a song that was very popular at the time in the *Yoshiwara*. And, with her nasal tones, The Lily sang,

Kyushu dai ichi no ume
Kon-ya kimi ga tame ni hiraku.
Hana no shingi wo shiran to hosseba
San-ko tsuki wo funde kitare.

It is such a beautiful song that I fear that I must translate it for you, for it gives an accurate picture of the feelings of The Lily at this particular time in her life. Also, it is the reason for a distinct turning point in her career. Translated it reads:

The finest plum-blossom of *Kyushu*

This night is opening for thee.
If thou wishest to know the true character
   of this flower,
Come at the hour of three, singing in the
   moonlight.

And all the while she was singing the song,
she was looking in the direction of the Prime
Minister, whose eyes were for no one but The
Lily but who could not voice his desire for her
because she was the guest of the Baron *Sochi*.
But when she came to the last line of the song,
she distinctly nodded her head to him and she
accented the hour of the rendezvous so that
he could not mistake her intentions; she was
singing the song expressly for him.

As she completed the song, The Lily bowed
gracefully. Then the music from the *samisens*
took on an entirely different tone. Something
animalistic crept into the music now. The six
geisha girls behind The Lily joined in the dance,
all in a row behind her. Weeping and wailing
like mad wantons in an orgy of sound, the
music came out of the instruments, the notes
tumbling over each other like a band of obscene
hokans.

Then they began to dance an Oriental dance
from the hips moving their arms and hands in
varied attitudes, twirling and swirling their
stomachs and their buttocks as though they
were each in the throes of great passion. Suddenly, in time with the music, they all cried
out, *"Chonkina!"* Four times they repeated this
word. Then, suddenly again, they all cried out,
"Hoi!" and, to the girl, they stopped instantly

still, not one muscle moving where, before, a thousand had quivered like a sea of gelatin. The idea of the dance was to determine which girl was the last one to become perfectly rigid. The loser then had to make a forfeit which, in this case, was the loss of some article of clothing. Here, the last girl to stop dropped her *obi* to the ground. This done, the *samisen* again took up their wail, the dancers twisted and squirmed every muscle in the bodies. The kimono of the girl who had lost the first round flapped open as her body swayed, displaying, at times, the delicious triangle of hair that covered her cunt. And every time this happened, the company of men would let out a roar of laughter and comment lewdly upon the scene. And the music continued, bringing the men to a passionate heat, even more than the sake they had swigged. Again *chonkina* was cried out by the girls. Again this was followed by *hoi*. And again they stopped and became rigid. The same girl who had lost before, lost again. This time, her kimono came off entirely. She was attired now in only a pair of aprons that came in front and behind her. Again the music took up the song. Again the *chonkina* and the *hoi*. Another girl lost the forfeit.

And so, on and on the music went until in time, all of the girls were stripped entirely naked. Now when they danced to the sensuous rhythms, the onlookers could see every muscle move. And their breasts shook like chaff in the wind. And their bellies moved around like a maelstrom of amylaceous flesh. And their buttocks whirled like windmills in the wind. And their cunnies flashed up and back and around and around like a madman's dream. And all the while the *samisens* strummed out their ecstatic song. And the odor of musk crept into the air. And the girls screwed up their faces as though they were already experiencing orgasm. And their fingers twitched with immodest gestures inviting the male to insert.

Suddenly the men could stand this no longer. Almost to the man, as though the same thought that prompted the one had prompted them all at the same moment, they leaped up drunkenly and swayed over to the girls. The Baron took hold of The Lily and, with her, sank down to one of the *kutons* that had been especially prepared for them. The other men had each chosen the girl that he desired and with them had likewise found themselves mattresses onto which they dragged the twittering *geisha*. The Prime Minister also chose a girl. But his eyes were always on The Lily. Even when he was drunkenly inserting his prick into his girl's cunt, he did not take his eyes from her but he watched her every movement and, as the Baron slowly stuck his prick into The Lily, he, the Prime Minister envied him and gave his prick a sharp poke which made the girl under him give a sharp cry of pain.

Thus, all over the floor, there were going on six grand fuckings. The air was filled with sighs and moans and cries from the *geisha* girls. And as the men grunted with passion and from exertion and out of mere drunkenness, the old *geisha* women in the background continued to strum their sensual *samisens*, grinning at the sexual antics of the couples on the floor, attempting to keep time by adjusting the rhythm of their songs to the rhythm of the pokes that the men were giving the girls.

The Lily, noticing that the Prime Minister had been watching her intently all the time, determined to give him a demonstration of her powers which would more than convince him of her superiority, insofar as expert fucking was concerned. And so, throwing herself heart and soul into the fucking she was getting from the Baron, she sweated herself mightily, demonstrating all of her varied arts, giving him more satisfaction than he had ever received in his life. Then, without shame, for women are peculiar in that respect and never demonstrate this talent where there are any others present, she took the Baron's limp prick into her mouth and tongued it like she had never tongued a prick before. Up and down over the entire length of the penis her agile tongue traveled. And at times she would give the skin a slight nip with her teeth accompanied by a slight tickling of her fingers at the base of his ball sac. Slowly but surely, the soft prick took on a hardness again. And again, with a loud roar, as though his sexual prowess was due to his own ability, the Baron threw himself onto The Lily. And quickly he poked his prick into her cunny.

And The Lily closed her eyes.

As she felt the Baron's prick warm her innards, she sighed. And she moaned. She threw her arms around his back. And she squeezed him mightily. She kissed him again and again on the mouth, each time forking her tongue into his mouth with the agility of a snake. And as she felt the Baron shoot off his hot sperm into her cunt and against her womb, she sighed.

For although it was the Baron on her body, it was the Prime Minister in her mind.

That orgy lasted far into the night.

And, the next evening, after she had rested completely from the exertions of the previous night, The Lily was lying in her bed on her belly while a blind shampooer kneaded his fingers into her tired muscles and brought life back to them. And as she lay on her *kuton*, her ears were given over to the sounds of footsteps in the hallway.

Soon, she was all attired for the night of joy. Her coiffure was piled up beautifully in her hair. The *kanzachi* were distributed in a tasteful aura around her head. Her face was not made up with the customary layer of white lacquer but glistened in the natural tints of her own fair skin. And her eyes gleamed with expectation. For she was expecting someone, the Prime Minister. Somehow or other she realized that he was going to call for her that night.

Outside, she heard the sounds of the street already taking life. The *gyu* from the various houses were filing down the stairs and into their cages. The venders of food filled the air with their raucous cries, *Jinriksha* men argued volubly as to the final amount they were to get for pulling their fares in from the city. In fact, to The Lily, these were all old sounds. What her ears were cocked for was a new sound, the sound of the Prime Minister's call for her.

One hour went by. Five men had sent up their demand for The Lily. On each of these occasions she had plead illness. There was only one man to whom she would go that night. And, as she smiled grimly to herself, she knew that the man would come, no matter what the hour would be.

But the hours flew by. The owner of the brothel was distraught. Twenty-five men had already asked for the services of The Lily. She had curtly refused all of them with the same pleas. She was sick. There was nothing for him to do. The rules of the *Yoshiwara* insisted that when a *yuyo* was ill, she was excused from active work for the night.

But the owner did not realize that The Lily was sick . . . she was lovesick. She was sick with love for the sturdy Prime Minister. She knew that in the Prime Minister there was what would be the acme of passion. He was one of the greatest men in the country. To be able to say that she had been fucked by the Prime Minister would be tantamount to saying that she had had the best. Finally, in desperation, because she did not believe in them, she decided to try to work one of the charms that the *yuyo* attempted in order to bring a wanted lover to their bed. First she tied two pillows together with her *obi* and flung them into an unlighted room. However, she felt foolish when she did this so she decided to try a more potent one. Taking equal parts of sake vinegar, *soy* oil, *chaguro*, with which the other *yuyo* blackened their teeth, water and a handful of *toshin* vegetable fiber lamp wicks, she boiled these seven ingredients together on the little stove in her room. To this potage she added a piece of paper on which she had previously drawn the prick and balls of her lover, the Prime Minister. Then she allowed this to boil again.

But still no Prime Minister came. In the night, as the cries of the street-sellers grew less, she heard the *Omon,* the great gate of the *Yoshiwara* being closed. She knew from that sound that the time was 10 o'clock. But she knew that even though the *Omon* was closed, the Prime Minister could still enter through the *kugurido,* a small door cut into the gate. At twelve o'clock, when the *Yoshiwara* was officially closed, she heard the *hyoshigi* wooden blocks being clapped together. And her hope fell. For she knew that now there would be little chance for the Prime Minister to come. And so, composing herself once more, she dismissed her *shinzo* and undressed herself and dropped to her *kuton.* For a while she could think of nothing but that she was disappointed in love. But, in time, like a fearful child, she fell off to sleep.

Of a sudden, in her sleep, she heard the sound of a song insinuating itself into her subconsciousness. For the moment, she allowed it to take its course, believing that it was only part and parcel of her dream. But something about the song was so real, too human, to be only the tenuous, ephemeral substance of a dream. And as she cautiously opened her eyes she expected the song to disappear with the dream at the same moment. But no, the dream disappeared but the song continued. It came from the corridor. The singer was at her door. It was a male voice and the voice was just completing the last line of the same popular *Yoshiwara* song that The Lily had sung at the banquet and orgy the night previous:

"San-ko tsuki who funde kitare."

The Lily caught her breath. From the clock in the tower of the highest building in the *Yoshiwara*, she heard the chimes boom out three times. It was three o'clock. The hour she had specified in her song. And now he is singing, "I come at the hour of three singing in the moonlight."

A ghostlike presence stole in silently through the door.

A wraith detached itself from the gloom and flung itself onto The Lily's *kuton*.

But it was a man who seized The Lily in his arms and kissed her eyelids and her hair and her lips and her breast in a mad ecstasy of passion.

It was the Prime Minister, *Kono Heima*.

"Why did you not come sooner, O my lover?" The Lily sobbed into his breath out of sheer joy.

"The Baron dogged my footsteps for hours, knowing that I had this rendezvous with three, O exquisite flower. But did not thy song name three as the hour? And is it not three?"

The Lily moaned. "Time is eradicated, o my honorable lover, when I am with thee! Three, four, eight, twelve, they all are only so many numbers! There is no time, only thee!" And, with these words, she began to disrobe her lover subtly while he continued to kiss her avidly on every part of her skin, being careful that he missed not even an iota. Soon, she had him completely naked with her. Then her hand went down to his prick. It was already distended but the moment her coiling fingers wrapped themselves tightly around its shaft, it seemed to take an extra spurt of inches. Lightly she stroked its length, knowing that for this first time, encouragement would hardly be necessary. Beneath its surface, in the veins, she could feel the life blood pulsing wildly through it, pumping hardness into its entire length, stiffening its contours until it almost took her breath away out of sheer anticipation of the thing.

And while she was fondling her lover's tool, the Prime Minister was not idle. His own hand was clutching and stroking her breasts, his fingers tipping her nipples at times while his other hand roamed down to her cunny, and, after skirmishing around for a moment, went into her pulsating hole and began to work on her already stiffening clitoris. Fiercely, her lips sought his lips. Fiercely, she opened her mouth wide so that it seemed that his lips seemed to have been swallowed entirely by her. But she seized hold of his tongue within her mouth and sucked it and nursed it and the essences of their mouths mingled as do the essences of the earth. And already they both felt that they were as one. Within each of their bodies there arose a strange, overweening desire for each other such as neither had ever felt before in their sexual lives. Almost without thought, each with a hand on the stiffened cock to direct its course, they brought it around to the entrance of her cunny. A delicious tingle went through them both when they each felt the hairs fronting her cunt come into contact with the prick's tip. And when the tip touched the outer lips of her warm, moist hole, a thrill went through them that almost made them both swoon into each other's arms. Electricity, the electricity of love, suffused them both until, like an electric battery, they were overcharged with it so that it poured out in great sparks at the least contact. Slowly, The Lily spread the lips of her cunny apart with one hand while, with the other, she helped her lover to direct his prick into her. First, she made certain that it scraped her already excited clitoris. And as she felt the entire length of prick rub up against that stiffened love button, she could not help but retract her guts merely out of the pleasure that it afforded her. And she drew her buttocks back at the same time. And, as the tip of his prick once more started its love journey into the cavern of her cunny, she gave a mighty thrust forward, swirling her hips at the same time so that the Prime Minister was forced to sink his tool to the hilt — so that he felt the hairs that lay around the bottom of his prick mingle with the hairs that protected his lover's grotto.

Back and forth now they each went. The sweat stood out on their foreheads like tiny bead pearls. Once The Lily nuzzled her nose under *Kono Heima's* armpit and sniffed mightily. "Tis like the essence of attar of roses," she gasped out to him. "Man-smell!" With these words, an overwhelming love for the man who had been in her already for some time came over her and she threw her arms around his chest and sank her fingernails deeply into his back out of sheer animal passion. And slowly, after that, she felt the seething within her at the pit of her loins, bubbling like the very fountain of life. And she twirled her ass the more. And she thrust her cunt back and forth with greater rapidity. And she seized hold of her lover's lips with greater ferocity. And she seemed to lose entire control of her senses.

At that same moment, she felt the floodgates within her give way to the tumultous surge of passion inside of her. And, at the same time, she felt the warm, moist splashing of the Prime Minister's sperm against the sides of her hot cunny. The odor of spilled semen pervaded the air. She sniffed it hungrily as a dog sniffs a corner. And she knew that she would not allow the prick that had caused her so much pleasure to leave the confines of her cunt so soon. And so, with the facility that she had acquired throughout her years at the *Yoshiwara*, she began to manipulate the sphincter muscles of her cunt while *Kono Heima's* prick was still reposing limp, in her cunt.

For the moment, he wondered what it was that was happening in her love spot. At first he thought it was the throbbing of his own member reacting to the fierce flood of passion that had gone through it. But no, there it was again, as though a ring of some soft material was tightening around his soft prick. Then he felt a slight tugging at it as though small hands were milking it and stretching it out.

Almost fearfully, he looked down at the juncture of their bodies at the point where their hairs mingled. There were no hands there, no mechanical contrivance of any sort. He looked down into the face of The Lily. "What is this that . . .?" But he said no more. For the answer to his unfinished question was written in the peculiar smile that was evident both around the corners of her eyes and her mouth. And, in answer to this, he sank his head down and kissed her on the lips and the neck and the ears, all over. And he almost sobbed in gratitude for the pleasure which she was affording him at that time. For already a feeling of revivified life was beginning to evidence itself in his prick. The marvelous tugging and sucking and milking of his prick continued with a continuous action.

Far into the night The Lily and her lover jousted thusly without a letup. Three, four and five times they fucked and, with each time, the Prime Minister vowed that he could do it no more, that his ambassador plenipotentiary was completely exhausted. But The Lily smiled her peculiar smile because she realized the capacity of her sexual prowess, and she set to work again after each fuck, sometimes milking his prick back to normalcy with her cunny muscles and at other times popping the limp penis into her mouth and licking it back into condition in that marvelous fashion of hers.

It is no wonder, then, that in the early hours of the morning, both of them fell into an exhausted sleep that lasted far into the afternoon hours of the next day. And, although a dozen messengers came dashing out to the *Yoshiwara* in impatient *jinrikshas* to implore the Prime

Minister that serious matters of state awaited his attention at the capital, nobody dared incur his wrath by awaking him. Once, the *kutsuwa* peeked into the door and saw the Prime Minister sleeping like a babe in the arms of The Lily, a beatific smile spread over his features. But the owner went no further. He backed away from the door and rubbed his hands. For he knew that this guest would need no encouragement from The Lily to leave *tsuri* for the housemen and, in fact, *sobana*, a large enough tip for the entire establishment from the *bantu* down to the meanest *wakaimono*, with an especially nice piece of change for the owner.

The Lily saw quite a bit of the Prime Minister after that. He too, like his predecessors, tried to inveigle her into leaving the *Yoshiwara* to become a concubine in his country house. But no amount of persuasion could jar The Lily loose from her determination to be free and on her own and able to choose a new man when the desire for it came over her. She knew that the life of a concubine was short and was determined by the time that it took her master to discover a newer and younger girl who was prettier than she and who was still unfucked.

It so happened that the Prime Minister was a wily fellow. His position close to the *Mikado's* ear had been quite secure up to this point. He had been the virtual ruler of Japan. For the *Mikado* was getting on in years and had begun to care less and less for the worries and troubles that were incident to governing the state. But the Prime Minister, *Kono Heima*, began to see, in the continued insistence of the

Crown Prince, the *Mikado's* son, to be allowed to take part in the state discussions, that his power over the throne would be lessened considerably were he not to get immediately into the good grace of the Crown Prince. And so, one evening, after they had gone into the affairs of the government and had begun to converse about that subject which usually crops up when men get together, women, the wily *Kono Heima* took the Crown Prince aside and told him of The Lily.

With lascivious gestures, he described each of her charms, going into detail about her private parts, telling him of the marvelous faculty that The Lily had for reviving the jaded spirits of a limp cock. And as the Prime Minister lingered on the details, he saw that the Crown Prince had become interested, for his eyes had begun to pop and he laved his lips with his tongue as though they were parched.

"Where is this paragon of woman you speak about, O honorable *Kono Heima?*" he asked.

"I shall bring her to your honorable highness," the Prime Minister replied, shaking a warning forefinger at his regent. "At the midnight hour, I shall bring her to your bed!" And, with these words, he chuckled to himself and shuffled away, shaking his head as though what he had just done was a huge joke.

Once again The Lily found herself being *jinrikshaed* out of the *Yoshiwara*. Her lover, the Prime Minister *Kono Heima*, had told her of a special mission that he had for her. Outside there was a *jinriksha* awaiting her arrival. "Dress well," he had informed her, "but over your apparel throw a black cloak so that none can recognize thee."

That was why she was in the *jinriksha*, being taken she knew not where by a *jinriksha* man who carried no *kemban* to light the way. This is a secret visit, she reasoned to herself as she settled back in the cushions. But as she turned to look back at the *Yoshiwara* when they had reached the *emon-zaka* hill, she saw the thousands of lanterns twinkling in the darkness. And a strange premonition came over her. She was about to direct the *jinriksha* man to turn back. For this premonition was that she was leaving the *Yoshiwara* forever. And that the looks she was now giving her home for the past five years were the last looks she would ever give it. And, involuntarily, tears came to her eyes. But she wiped the tears away and settled back into the cushions. And breathed the cool night air mingled with the clean odor of pines and cherry blossoms. She almost lulled herself to sleep watching the hypnotic, rhythmic action of the *jinriksha* man's legs pumping up and down as he ran steadily onward down the road that led back to the city.

This time, however, she did not pass through the poorer section as she had done on her last visit. Beautiful mansions lined the road until finally, they pulled up to an enormous structure of magnificent external appearance.

"Where are we?" The Lily whispered to the *jinriksha* man.

He shook his head and drew up to the rear of the place.

From out of the shadows stepped a figure.

195

The Lily shrank but she took heart again when she saw that it was only *Kono Heima* swathed in a long black cloak. She was about to ask him the reason for all this secrecy, but he stopped her with a finger to his lips, taking her by the waist and whisking her into the open doorway and up a magnificent flight of stairs. Then, taking her hand, he led her into a bedroom. The Lily saw that it was the *zishiki* of a very wealthy man. For the woodwork was like brown satin and the matting glistened almost as though it were lacquered. Fine painted screens with gold backgrounds were scattered around while, on the walls, were distributed original paintings of the master Japanese artists. Objects of art were tastefully placed in the various alcoves. But, most aristocratic of all, there reclined in a wonderfully brocaded *kuton*, a young man whose bearing, even in his reclining position, was quite evident.

The Prime Minister, a smug, complacent smirk on his face, bowed low to the person on the bed of mattresses. "Bow low!" he whispered to The Lily. "Bow low to thy Crown Prince!"

The Lily stared at the Crown Prince. A hard look came into her eyes at first, a look of disgust because of the despicable actions of her one-time lover who was now selling her for the favors of the throne. But she smiled again when she realized that she was rising in the ladder of life to being the mistress of the soon-to-be *Mikado* of Japan. And she bowed low.

"Here is the beauty from the *Yoshiwara* that I promised your honorable highness," *Kono Heima* said slowly.

196

The Crown Prince waved the Prime Minister away airily, with a languid finger, and *Kono Heima* backed out of the room, leaving The Lily alone with the Prince.

Again the Prince waved his finger languidly, beckoning for The Lily to advance forward to his *kuton*. She did so. His hand went under her kimono and sought her cunny. For a while, he felt around it. Then, apparently satisfied, he drew her down to him on the *kuton* and disrobed her completely. Still he said no word. Then, spreading her legs apart, he jockeyed himself into position between her thighs in front of her cunt and stuck a very emaciated penis into her. Immediately The Lily thought back to the time when she had taken on the little son of the *kutsuwa* of the first brothel she had worked in. The Crown Prince's prick felt like the boy's little penis had felt, like a little worm wriggling inside of her. Suddenly, before she could complete the thought, she felt something warm inside her. The prince had already come into her. The little worm shriveled up again into nothing. Then with a sigh of ennui, he lifted himself up and away from her and, turning over on his side, composed himself for sleep.

The Lily was stunned. Never before had this happened. Here a man had been in her, more than a man, a crown prince. He had been satisfied only to stir her faintly and then, without a word of warning, had spurted his semen into her and then gone to sleep. When she finally realized what had happened, she gently tugged at the Prince's arm.

He tried to shake her off. "Let me alone!" he complained.

"But you have not really had me yet!" she insisted.

"I'm sleepy!" he yawned.

"But I would have thee really fuck me!" she insisted, and, worming her arm around his hips, she tried to take hold of his tiny prick. But she could not find it, so small was it and so imbedded was it in his pubic hair. "Let me alone, woman!" he complained imperiously. "I have had thee once. That is sufficient to myself!" After that he said no more but, directly, in a few minutes was snoring blissfully in sleep.

Here was a situation that The Lily had never before had to cope with. Always the men with whom she had slept were avid for contact with her. And the more she could rouse them to fuck, the better they liked her for it. Yet, here was a thing that called itself a man and a crown prince who pushed her away angrily.

For a while, she lay next to the Prince and composed her thoughts. She heard the snore of the man next to her and it grated on her ears, like the squeak of a saw. For in her there burned that desire for man that the Prince had only served to awaken. In her there seethed that itch to be fucked recklessly, spontaneously, with all the strength and vivacity and virility that could be gotten up.

But there was no man to take her.

And so, about an hour later, she got up out of bed and, donning her night kimono, she stepped out into the spacious hall and walked its length in order to walk down the yearning in her. Suddenly she heard the soft pad of footsteps coming down the wide sweep of stairs at the extreme end of the corridor. Breathlessly, she stood in her tracks and awaited the newcomer. A figure appeared at the bottom of the stairs. It was an old man, his face seamed and wrinkled, his knees bowed from the weight of years.

He peered down the corridor, his eyes sunk deeply beneath gray eyebrows. "Who is it that prowls around like a lone wolf?" he inquired as he advanced to The Lily, shivering in her nightrobe.

She stood speechless.

The old man looked her over as he advanced. "What is thy name, woman, and what are you doing here?" he demanded.

Something majestically regal about the old man held her from answering at first. But finally she found her tongue and told him her name. "I was brought here for the Crown Prince's pleasure!" she told him, her voice quivering from fear.

"For my son?" the old man asked, "that stick?"

Immediately, The Lily sank to her knees, her head bowed almost to the ground for she realized that she was in the presence of the Emperor of Japan, the *Mikado!*

"I know why you walk the night here instead of gracing my son's bed as you should!" he said to her kindly now, and he bent and took her by the elbow and lifted her graciously to her feet. "My son is scarcely a man, the fool!" he spat out, "and it is that which is to rule

Japan!" He caught himself. "But you are a beautiful woman!" He peered into her face now, his eyes almost touching her nose. "Who are you?" he insisted. "Have I not seen you before?"

The Lily shook her head.

The old man again peered into her face. Then he shook his head. "I am certain that I have seen you!" A thin, quizzical smile came into his face. "I am dreaming," he continued, "for I have not been with a woman these past five years. That is why my bed was so cold and why I am walking these corridors." He laughed as though to himself. "We are a frigid pair, my son and I," he grinned. Then, suddenly, a thought came to him. "Come, my child, come to my bed. Perhaps your young, hot-blooded body might warm my cold limbs somewhat!" And, taking her arm, he led her up the stairs from whence he had come, on past a cordon of men who gasped when they saw what it was that their *Mikado* was leading, and into an enormous bedroom, even more richly furnished than had been the bedroom of the Prince she had just vacated.

The *Mikado* dropped stiffly to the *kuton*, groaning as old men groan, when his bones creaked. "Doff your robe," he told her, "so that I might gain full benefit of your warmth."

She did as she was bade, her naked, slim body standing out in the moonlight like an alabaster statue. The *Mikado* stared hungrily at her. "What a feast for a younger man!" he said, "while I must be content to sate my passion with food!" Again he eyed her in all her glorious nakedness. "By all the saints!" he swore, "if I do not feel a strange ache in my loins for you!" And, saying this, he seized her wrist and dragged her down onto the *kuton* with him.

The Lily felt his cold limbs up against her own warm body. And, somehow, instead of being revolted by the old man, an odd feeling of pity came over her. And she threw her arms around the old man's thin body and drew him close to hers.

"I am beginning to feel warmer!" the old man cried. "Who are you?" And, becoming over-joyed, he snuggled closer to her, like a child snuggles closer to its mother on a cold morning. The Lily felt for his prick. It was a shriveled and emaciated one. But she could feel that, despite its softness, it had once reveled night after night in fuckfests.

"Tis the tool of an old man," the *Mikado* said sadly, "but once it could prance with the best of them, not like my son!" he added ruefully.

But The Lily was not listening to his chatter. Instead, she was busying herself with the hardening of the flaccid thing that was in her hands. Expertly, she kissed the soft tip and flicked along the sides with her tongue, kissing it at timed intervals. But it appeared that there was no use. The old man's prick was simply fucked out. And, although she had managed to revivify the desire in him for it, still, although the spirit was willing the flesh was weak, very weak.

But she popped the thing into her mouth and sucked it and milked it and stroked its sides with her tongue and tickled his balls. So that, after some time, wonder of all wonders, signs of life began to show in the bewrinkled penis. "What have you done to me, woman?" the *Mikado* inquired as he felt blood surge once more into his member. "Have you performed a miracle?" And he dropped his hand to his prick to feel a hitherto unaccustomed hardness in it. Then, before he could realize it, he felt The Lily swarming over him, her mouth kissing him blindly on the mouth, on the eyes, all over his body. He seized hold of The Lily's breasts and fondled them and felt their nipples rising like soldiers to their duty. And, sending his hand down to her cunny, he inserted his fingers to find a strange quivering there. He fingered her clitoris and found that member standing stiffly at attention, also ready for action.

Then it happened.

Taking the old man's quasi-stiffened penis into her hand, she spread her legs wide and, directing the course of the prick, she stuck its head past the outer lips of her vagina, on past the clitoris and partially into her quivering quim, as far as the hardness of the prick would allow.

"What now?" the *Mikado* cried. "It's too late. I cannot make it any harder!"

But, before he completed the sentence, something within him stiffened. Something was happening to him. For, around his limp prick, he felt a thousand small fingers busily stroking his member, tugging at the loose skin, sucking the very essence from him. A ring of iron tightened around his penis with timed seizures while the hands continued to milk him. But something in his mind was disturbing him. And despite the

joy that he felt in seeing himself raised to a
hard-on once more, after a lapse of five years,
a curious fear was gathering at the back of his
brain. But the exigencies of the fuck were
strong enough to drive those thoughts into the
background for the time being. And he gave
himself now wholeheartedly over to the antics
of the marvelous woman beneath him. And he
felt his penis take on a hardness such as it
had not experienced for years. And, sensing the
movements of The Lily, he began to direct his
cock back and forth into the hot aperture that
the woman had prepared for him. And the
tears came to his eyes out of the sheer joy in
the knowledge that life had been brought back
to him for a moment, even though it was the
last spurt, like the last spurt of life in a dying
man or the last flicker from a dying candle.
And, within him, he felt his loins boil. And he
felt that he could hold himself no longer. And
he spurted his last load of semen into The Lily's
cunt and sank backwards to the cushions, entirely exhausted and panting with passion.

*   *   *

It was then that the thoughts that he had
managed to push into the background returned.
Something there was about this woman that
was reminiscent of another woman whom he
had fucked many years ago. That was it. She,
too, had had that marvelous faculty of being
able to milk his prick while it was still soft and
still in her cunt. And, strangely, now that he
cast his mind's eye back to her, she had looked

like the woman who was under him now. That was why she appeared to be someone he had met before when he had accosted her in the corridor.

Then the awful thought struck him.

And he recoiled as though he had been struck a blow between the eyes.

"Why do you shudder so?" The Lily asked him.

He opened his eyes slowly. Then he stared over her face, searching every line for a sign of recognition. Yes, it was she! it was one of his former concubines! "Who was your mother, child?" he asked her slowly. She told him. She scarcely recalled her mother. She knew only that she was once a member of the court.

At these words, the *Mikado* let out a shriek of pain, a cry that was pitiful and horrible at the same time. Yes. He knew it. No other woman had been able to milk him as that old one had.

This girl was her daughter.

This girl was his daughter.

He had fucked his own daughter.

He had committed incest.

* * *

The *Yoshiwara* saw no more of The Lily after that. She disappeared completely from sight. Rewards were offered for her return. Much ado was made about her kidnaping. But she never returned to public life. Not even the Prime Minister knew what happened to her. He was discreet enough to keep his mouth closed, for he thought that the Crown Prince had done away with her.

But he often wondered why the *Mikado* had commissioned him to build a solitary castle in the countryside miles away from the city. And he never connected this odd fact with the disappearance of The Lily.

And on the door of The Lily's room, a grieving poet inscribed the words:

> *O-bune no*
> *Hatsuru-tomari no*
> *Tayutai ni*
> *Mono-omoi-yase-nu*

With a rocking
As of great ships
Riding at anchor
She has at last become worn out with love.

THE END

MORE EROTIC CLASSICS FROM
CARROLL & GRAF

☐ Anonymous/ALTAR OF VENUS	$3.95
☐ Anonymous/ANGELICA	$3.95
☐ Anonymous/AUTOBIOGRAPHY OF A FLEA	$3.95
☐ Anonymous/THE CELEBRATED MISTRESS	$3.95
☐ Anonymous/CONFESSIONS OF AN ENGLISH MAID	$3.95
☐ Anonymous/CONFESSIONS OF EVELINE	$3.95
☐ Anonymous/COURT OF VENUS	$3.95
☐ Anonymous/THE COURTESAN	$3.95
☐ Anonymous/DANGEROUS AFFAIRS	$3.95
☐ Anonymous/THE DIARY OF A MATA HARI	$3.95
☐ Anonymous/DOLLY MORTON	$3.95
☐ Anonymous/THE EDUCATION OF A MAIDEN	$3.95
☐ Anonymous/THE EROTIC READER	$3.95
☐ Anonymous/THE EROTIC READER II	$3.95
☐ Anonymous/FANNY HILL'S DAUGHTER	$3.95
☐ Anonymous/FLORENTINE AND JULIA	$3.95
☐ Anonymous/A LADY OF QUALITY	$3.95
☐ Anonymous/LENA'S STORY	$3.95
☐ Anonymous/LOVE PAGODA	$3.95
☐ Anonymous/THE LUSTFUL TURK	$3.95
☐ Anonymous/MADELEINE	$3.95
☐ Anonymous/A MAID'S JOURNEY	$3.95
☐ Anonymous/MAID'S NIGHT IN	$3.95
☐ Anonymous/THE MEMOIRS OF JOSEPHINE	$3.95
☐ Anonymous/MICHELE	$3.95
☐ Anonymous/PLEASURE'S MISTRESS	$3.95
☐ Anonymous/PRIMA DONNA	$3.95
☐ Anonymous/ROSA FIELDING: VICTIM OF LUST	$3.95
☐ Anonymous/SECRET LIVES	$3.95
☐ Anonymous/THREE TIMES A WOMAN	$3.95
☐ Anonymous/VENUS DELIGHTS	$3.95
☐ Anonymous/VENUS DISPOSES	$3.95

☐	Anonymous/VENUS IN INDIA	$3.95
☐	Anonymous/VENUS IN PARIS	$3.95
☐	Anonymous/VENUS REMEMBERED	$3.95
☐	Anonymous/VENUS UNBOUND	$3.95
☐	Anonymous/VENUS UNMASKED	$3.95
☐	Anonymous/VICTORIAN FANCIES	$3.95
☐	Anonymous/THE WANTONS	$3.95
☐	Anonymous/A WOMAN OF PLEASURE	$3.95
☐	Anonymous/WHITE THIGHS	$4.50
☐	Perez, Faustino/LA LOLITA	$3.95
☐	van Heller, Marcus/ADAM & EVE	$3.95
☐	van Heller, Marcus/THE FRENCH WAY	$3.95
☐	van Heller, Marcus/THE HOUSE OF BORGIA	$3.95
☐	van Heller, Marcus/THE LIONS OF AMON	$3.95
☐	van Heller, Marcus/ROMAN ORGY	$3.95
☐	van Heller, Marcus/VENUS IN LACE	$3.95
☐	Villefranche, Anne-Marie/FOLIES D'AMOUR	$3.95
	Cloth	$14.95
☐	Villefranche, Anne-Marie/JOIE D'AMOUR	$3.95
	Cloth	$13.95
☐	Villefranche, Anne-Marie/PLAISIR D'AMOUR	$3.95
	Cloth	$12.95
☐	Von Falkensee, Margarete/BLUE ANGEL NIGHTS	$3.95

Available from fine bookstores everywhere or use this coupon for ordering:

Caroll & Graf Publishers, Inc., 260 Fifth Avenue, N.Y., N.Y. 10001

Please send me the books I have checked above. I am enclosing
$_____ (please add $1.75 per title to cover postage and
handling.) Send check or money order—no cash or C.O.D.'s
please. N.Y. residents please add 8¼% sales tax.

Mr/Mrs/Miss _____

Address _____

City _____ State/Zip _____

Please allow four to six weeks for delivery.